MURDER MOST BEASTLY

MELISSA CLEARY

BERKLEY PRIME CRIME, NEW YORK

MURDER MOST BEASTLY

A Berkley Prime Crime Book / published by arrangement with the author

PRINTING HISTORY
Berkley Prime Crime edition / January 1996

ISBN: 0-425-15139-5

Berkley Prime Crime Books are published
by The Berkley Publishing Group,
200 Madison Avenue, New York, NY 10016.
The name BERKLEY PRIME CRIME and the BERKLEY PRIME CRIME
design are trademarks belonging to Berkley Publishing Corporation.

PRINTED IN THE UNITED STATES OF AMERICA

10 9 8 7 6 5 4 3 2 1

MURDER MOST BEASTLY

When Jane Bellamy, a civil planning teacher from Rodgers University, became the mayor of Palmer, defeating the somewhat corrupt Bill Curtis, she managed to persuade the City Council to devote a certain portion of the city's taxes to remodeling the Palmer Zoo into the Palmer Wildlife Habitat Park. The changes were superficial, but the publicity was not. This was fortunate for Morton Slake, a former councilman who had been swept out along with Mayor Curtis, who then became the head of the Palmer Wildlife Habitat. When the public heard the story that Irv, the second-oldest gorilla in captivity, had fathered a little guy named Gooey, the Wildlife Habitat became the feel-good story of the hour. Unfortunately, any chance of receiving national or international publicity quickly went by the boards when the only gorilla in captivity older than Irv, a mean, sloppy-looking guy in the Atlanta Zoo, rose to the challenge and fathered a baby as well.

The citizens of Palmer, irked by another failure, then turned away from the Palmer Wildlife Habitat with a vengeance and Mort Slake and his staff and their wards slipped back into obscurity.

The one zookeeper in the Wildlife Habitat Park who really seemed to love animals simply for themselves was Grover Gilmore. The son of Thalia Gilmore, an activist involved in the care of dogs and the promotion of their rights, Grover had worked in the Palmer Zoo in its various incarnations for nearly twenty years. In the last several years, Grover had become increasingly worried about the state of the zoo and had begun cautiously looking for an outlet to share his dismay with the public at large. Grover wanted to tell people that for several years he had been watching lazy and inefficient park management result in the mistreatment and the early demise of several of the animals. Unable to provoke the City Council into doing something about it, Grover had finally gone to the local television station. It was Grover's hope that KCIN's crusading anchorwoman, Marcella Jacobs, would look into the matter.

Now, as he worked quietly alone in the Aviary-Simian House after hours, Grover wondered if he had done the right thing. After all, someone was killing the animals. Maybe, if they found out that Grover and Marcella were investigating them, they would switch to human beings.

CHAPTER 1

Little figures, Peter thought to himself with some satisfaction. *Is there any more perfect way in the world to spend your life than in painting little figures?*

"And the answer is *no!*" Peter assured his dog, in conscious imitation of his father's favorite talk show host.

As Peter Walsh, a solid—well, chunky—young hockey player for Palmer's Downtown Arts School and the son of Rodgers University's favorite film instructor and amateur sleuth extraordinaire, methodically separated his new lead skeleton army, he thought to himself, *Things couldn't be better!*

To celebrate, Peter flattened out the box the skeletons had come in and Frisbeed it across the room, knocking the things-to-do list his mother had left him back behind his desk where he'd never have to think of it again.

"Pretty good, hunh, Jake?"

Peter's companion, a German shepherd who had once worked as a canine officer for the Palmer Po-

lice Department, just gave his mistress's son a disgusted look.

Never mind, Peter thought to himself. Heck, he
wasn't going to let some dumb old dog ruin his good
time. Especially on a perfect day like this one was
turning out to be.

Why was this, of all days, perfect? Well, first of all,
Peter had the entire afternoon just to goof off. All
the snow they had been getting this year had
blocked off the roads to the fieldhouse where Peter's hockey team skated, so practice had been canceled again.

To some, it would probably be ironic that hockey
practice was going to be canceled because of snowy
weather, but not to young Peter Walsh. No intellec-
tual was he—and damn proud of it. As far as Peter
was concerned, irony was something they put into
multivitamins to make his mom buy them.

Peter now took the little plastic holder the skeleton army had come in and punted it with the well-
bruised toe of his hundred-and-fifty-dollar sneaker.

"Score!" he yelled, as the holder knocked over
the furniture polish can his mother had left on his
bureau as an unsubtle hint to do a little room cleaning.

Jake, burdened by the knowledge of how his beloved mistress would cringe if she saw this scene un-
folding, put his paws up over his eyes.

"Ha, ha!" Peter gloated. The truth was, he was
proud of himself. For once in his short life, Peter
had managed to talk his Irish-American grandmother, Frances Costello, into giving him some of

her poker winnings, instead of some dorky clothes from Gap Kids. Once he had gotten his hands on the loot, Peter had carefully invested his birthday lucre in an expensive set of plastic figures called the Teen Skater Hall of Villains Silver Skeleton Strike Force and had managed to keep enough left over to hire his pal Isaac Cook to shovel his sidewalk.

As far as Peter Walsh was concerned, there was no smarter seventh grader in the history of mankind, and he was about to repeat that to Jake the Great when all of a sudden the phone rang.

"Drat!" Peter said loudly. If he were alone he would have used a harsher, more locker-room expression, but Jake hated cursing and often nipped him if he swore too volubly.

Why his mother didn't get another phone answering machine, Peter didn't know. It wasn't his fault it got broke that time when he was practicing chip shots in the hallway. Peter pried open his bedroom door with a sigh and staggered out into the hall.

Boy was he stiff. Lying around all the time will do that to you.

Finally, Peter managed to slide down the banister to the first floor, accidentally knocking his mother's stupid Minute Man lamp over. Once again, Peter had been saved only by his lightning-fast reflexes from being seriously hurt by a trap left for him by a thoughtless mother. It was almost more than he could bear sometimes, but enough self-pity—there was a phone to answer.

"Yeah?" he grunted.

"Peter?" a familiar voice greeted him.

"Yeah," Peter conceded.

"This is Marcella, Peter."

"I know," he replied. What did Palmer's local TV newsperson take him for, anyway? Stupid?

"Is your mother home, dear?"

"Nope," he responded laconically. Peter often fancied himself as a younger, stockier Clint Eastwood, with different-colored hair and a rounder jaw.

"Do you expect her?"

"She's gotta come home sometime." Peter vaguely remembered that his mother had given him some information about what she was going to do this afternoon and when she was returning home, but because he had been sleeping when she started yelling stuff at him through his closed bedroom door, he didn't remember a word of it.

"Well," Marcella continued, raising her voice over some background noise, "tell her I called. And have her call me on my cellular phone as soon as she gets in. It's very important. All right?"

"Whatever you say," Peter shrugged. Grown-ups were always telling you something that was very important. But was it really very important? No, siree. Usually it was quite boring, frankly.

"Would you write that down for me?" Marcella requested politely. The gruff-voiced former newspaper reporter usually yelled at people to get results, but with difficult young adolescent boys like Peter she could be very charming.

"Yeah, all right," Peter grudgingly conceded. It was a wonder he had any energy left at all anymore, the way people gave him stuff to do.

Taking the grease pencil his mother had tied to the message board near the phone, he wrote on his arm, "Mom. Call Marsella."

Peter was a master war game strategist. Not a speller.

"Got it."

"Thank you, Peter," Marcella said sweetly. "How have you been lately, sugar?"

The reference to sugar clicked off little bells in Peter's brain. If memory served him correctly, there were some sweets in the cupboard, hidden behind his mother's oven mitts. "Okay, I guess." He then came up with a fiendish way to turn this boring conversation to his own advantage. "Hey, Marcy. Guess what."

"What, dear?"

"It's my birthday soon."

"How wonderful. How old are you going to be?"

"Old enough," he answered blithely.

"Well, great!"

"Are you going to get me anything?" Peter asked.

"Of course," Marcella answered. "What would you like?"

"Well, you know what would be good?" Peter said at once. "If you got me those skeleton horses, you know, the ones that go with the skeleton army? Not the *red* skeleton army that has the cauldrons where they're burning the babies," Peter carefully specified, knowing what sort of atrocities could happen if you didn't lay out for grown-ups chapter and verse. "The *silver* skeleton army. The really cool ones . . ."

All of a sudden, the line, with an ominous click, went dead.

Bummer, Peter thought to himself. Now he wouldn't know for sure whether she was going to get him the right horses or not. *Oh, well, you can't win 'em all.* Then, scratching himself with rueful self-knowledge, Peter went into the kitchen for a much-needed snack.

CHAPTER 2

"Isn't this great?" Jackie asked, rubbing her hand delightedly over what seemed to be a cosmetics case.

Jackie Walsh was the curly-haired mother of young Peter Walsh. Unaware that her friend Marcella's portable telephone had mysteriously cut out, Jackie was currently in her small office in the Longacre Communications Center at Rodgers University, where she gave two film history lectures, showed films, and taught a filmmaking lab each week.

"It's very nice. What is it?" asked Ronald Dunn, Jackie's actor-boyfriend.

"A pet suitcase." Jackie opened the top and flipped down the side so they could inspect the interior. "Pretty nifty, right?" Jackie proudly displayed the compartments, straps, and pockets that held grooming supplies, medicines, food, water, towels, leashes, and even . . .

Ron furrowed his perfectly tanned patrician brow as he contemplated a strange telescoping aluminum device with a flat mini-snow shovel on the end. "A pooper scooper?"

"Bingo!" Jackie beamed. She loved having an intelligent romantic partner for a change. While her former husband Cooper and her former boyfriend Michael were not stupid, exactly, they certainly did not hold doctorates as Ronald Dunn did. "Would you mind putting this in your car?"

"Glad to," the former television spy responded. "May I ask—were you planning to bring Jake along to the airport?"

Jackie and Dunn had been trying to get away to Florida for a brief holiday for some months.

"Actually, I was planning to bring Jake along on the trip. Is that a problem?" Jackie asked. So busy had Jackie been lately that she had had very little time to spend with Jake.

"It's not a problem for me," Dunn said at once, brushing an imaginary speck of lint off his immaculate charcoal-gray Versace pants. "But won't Jake be a little cramped for space in my BMW?"

The aforementioned Jake was in point of fact a large dog, some four and a half feet long, approximately three feet high, and weighing nearly a hundred sixty pounds. Still, he was more than just a dog. A brilliant K-9 detective who had been instructed by the late trainer, Cornelius Mitchell, Jake had come to the Walsh family after he had been wounded by a bullet. Since that time, Jake had performed heroically in guarding the Walshes against intruders and in helping Jackie solve crimes that stumped the Palmer Police Department.

Jackie replied, "I suppose he would, wouldn't he? I was going to leave my Jeep here, in case my neigh-

bor Merida needed it to take Peter somewhere.''
She then looked at her watch and announced, "Oh,
I can't think right now, Ron. I have to go down to
the auditorium and give my four o'clock lecture.
We'll work out the arrangements later.''

"All right," Dunn amiably agreed. "Just tell me
when you want me to book airline tickets. I can handle it through my laptop modem.''

"Gosh, ain't technology wonderful," Jackie lied.
She kissed Ron on the cheek and headed for her
locker. "The thing is, now I'm worried about taking
Jake on the plane.''

"I'm sure those baggage compartments are plenty
big enough," Ron assured Jackie, helping her on
with her cardigan.

"It's not the space issue I'm worried about,"
Jackie replied, running a brush quickly through her
hair. She tossed Dunn the newsletter that she had
received from her friend Thalia's Canine Rights
Lobby every month.

"What am I looking at?" Dunn asked.

"The article right there on the front page,"
Jackie said impatiently. "It says that seventy animals
died last year traveling in baggage compartments—
mostly from suffocation or heat stroke.''

Dunn shook his head in sympathy.

"I know, I know. Chances are, even though the
luggage compartments are unheated, uncooled, and
unpressurized, nothing will happen. But I don't see
why I should take that chance.''

"Who's asking you to?" Dunn asked, taking Jackie

in his arms. "Maybe we could buy Jake a seat or something."

Jackie allowed herself to be kissed, then offered a kiss of her own so as not to seem like a bad sport. "Maybe. But then when we get to Florida, we'd have to drive around in a rental car."

"We'll get the best car money can rent," Dunn promised.

"We'll get an electric car," Jackie reminded her boyfriend.

"Oh, yeah," he remembered. They separated, their ardor cooled by the prospect of tooling around in one of the small, sluggish electric battery-powered cars that states like Florida, Massachusetts, and California were testing in their rental car programs, as possible replacements for the fossil-fuel burners that now ruled the roads.

"What if I drive the Jeep to Florida?" Jackie proposed suddenly.

"Would you mind?"

"Not me. I love to drive."

"Great. And if you get tired, I'll take a shift now and then." Dunn then laughed as he saw the set of Jackie's jaw. She was willing to share a lot of things with him, but not, apparently, the driving of her Jeep.

Jackie then caught sight of the giant wristwatch clock, hung to one side of her Mae West poster. "Yikes!" she exclaimed. "I'm late."

"See you tonight," Dunn said quickly, grabbing up the pet suitcase and his own script folder. The veteran actor was rehearsing for a special encore performance on the *Golden Biscuit Hour,* a weekly radio program broadcast over the airwaves of Rodgers's own KJRD.

"Dinner?" Jackie asked, picking up her own briefcase and making sure that her lecture notes were inside.

"Sure," Dunn agreed at once. "Charley's?"

Jackie nodded, then posed, kissing the tips of her fingers before using them to wave "au revoir." "I'll see you at seven then, Pepe . . ."

Dunn smiled at Jackie's husky-voiced imitation of Hedy Lamarr and responded in a flawless Charles Boyer, "Then, *ma chérie,* I will see you in my dreams."

CHAPTER 3

Pissed off that her expensive phone had cut out on her without warning *again*, Marcella Jacobs, Palmer's premier investigative television reporter, looked in the mirror and made a face.

"What's the matter?" Grover Gilmore asked.

"I look like Shemp Howard," Marcella replied. It was true. The tall, fashionably thin, golden-blond anchorwoman looked goofy in the black wig that she had allowed herself to be talked into wearing as a disguise.

"We should get upstairs," Grover worried.

Growling like one of the beasts she was about to tend, Marcella slowly rose up from her seat. "This better be the best story I've ever covered, Gilmore."

"Don't worry," the veteran City of Palmer Parks Department employee assured her. "It's a corker."

Looking and feeling clunky in her belted blue coveralls and steel-toe reinforced work boots, Marcella looked around the ugly locker room. The cracked and peeling plaster walls were papered with Scotch tape-reinforced pictures of animals and ex-

otic climes, torn out of half-price calendars and
magazines, but it didn't do much to cheer the place
up.

Leaving the locker room, Marcella climbed the
cement steps to the cold room above, wondering
how it was that she had been talked into this goofy
gig. Grover was kind of cute, but now that Marcella
had a boyfriend, she was less inclined to select stories on the basis of hormones. Was what had happened at the Palmer Wildlife Habitat really that
bad? Grover had given her a list of particulars which
he now planned to illustrate. It certainly had
sounded to Marcella like the number of animals
that had died in the last year and a half was excessive, but who was she to say? The real reason that
she had followed this story, Marcella decided, was
that she had a feeling that what was going on in the
Palmer Wildlife Habitat was somehow mixed up
with Jane Bellamy and her crew. For weeks there
had been murmurs that Palmer's controlling oligar-
chy, the people who ran the bottled water concerns,
the snack-food makers, the soda-pop bottlers, and
most of the land in town, had been meeting in various places under various guises, obviously up to
something. Marcella just hoped that the something
they were planning had something to do with this
zoo.

"Cold, hunh?" Grover asked her.

"Yeah, it sure is." This particular area was where
the perishable food for the animals was stored.

Opening a large brown-paper-wrapped drum of
chilled hamburger meat was a young man whom

Marcella immediately recognized. It was Hoss Greenaway, heir to a bottled beverage fortune. His parents believed that he shouldn't have anything handed to him, so Hoss had been bouncing from one miserable low-paying job to another as his father tried futilely to instill in his awkward son a work ethic that would one day allow him to run his mother's company.

Marcella averted her head and was happy to see that the young lad's thick eyeglasses had steamed up in the cold room.

"Who's that?" Hoss asked in a high-pitched voice.

"It's Grover, Hoss," Marcella's guide said affably Then, moving between young Hoss and Marcella, Grover helped to further shield his undercover guest from the hardworking employee's nearsighted gaze. "You know, uh, Carly, don't you? She's the new animal keeper."

"New, hunh? Hey, that's great," Hoss said at once. "I've only been working here a couple of months—ever since I got fired from the pizza place."

Marcella felt bad. It was, after all, her dog Maury—now chained to a post in the parking lot—that was the bottomless-bellied beast that had caused young Hoss to get fired.

"Pleased to meet you . . ." Marcella said finally, trying for a slightly nasal Long Island, New York, accent.

"Hoss!" the young Greenaway lad responded. "Hoss Greenaway. You've probably heard of my father, Max?"

"No," Marcella lied.

"Oh, well," Hoss chattered on, a bit startled. It was the first time he had ever talked to someone who didn't know who his father was. He thought people like that were confined to China. "He's been helping my mother run her soda-pop business lately. He's got these cool ads running on TV. You've probably seen them."

"No," Marcella lied again. Marcella didn't know why she was denying even the fact that she watched the local advertisements on television, but, she figured, better safe than sorry when you're working undercover.

"Anyway," Hoss continued, "I started working here late last year and I really like it."

"Great," Marcella said with an air of dismissing him.

"And there's no better old hand to show you the ropes than Grover Gilmore here. Take it from a guy who knows . . ." Hoss then turned away to sneeze. "Man, it's cold in here."

"Try those vitamin C supplements like I told you, Hoss," Grover admonished, edging Marcella toward the exit.

Ignoring his boss, Hoss continued, "Listen, Carly . . ."

Marcella turned her famous glare of death on the young zookeeper, hoping to laser him silent.

It didn't work.

"I don't suppose," Hoss proposed, "you would ever consider going out to the best restaurant in town with me?"

Marcella knew that on some level she should be flattered that even looking hideous as she did, one of the richest young men in town should be hitting on her. On the other hand, Marcella was used to the protection that being an attractive celebrity afforded her—namely that young men like Hoss Greenaway would never hit on someone like her, knowing it would not only be pointless, but indeed an insult to waste the time of such a beauty.

So she got mad.

"No, I would never consider that," she said sharply.

"Carly has a boyfriend," Grover explained to Hoss, trying to take him off the hook.

"Well . . . if you ever break up with him," Hoss countered, "give me a call."

Hoss did not have to kid himself, but since it was easier all the way around, he always did.

Grover then opened the heavy door to the outside. "Well, Hoss. I'm going to show Carly around. See you later."

"Bye!" Marcella said shortly.

"See ya, Grover!" Hoss yelled back. "See you, Carly!"

As the animal keeper went back to his work, plucking out chunks of semifrozen meat and throwing them on a wheelbarrow, Grover turned back to Marcella.

"Well, you're just the newest in an ever-changing kaleidoscope of new faces, Carly," Grover informed the newswoman as they walked.

"Really?" Marcella responded without interest.

She was now counting the minutes until she had the four or five facts she needed for a fifteen-minute story.

"Yeah," Grover continued. "This is a city-owned Wildlife Habitat Park, so every time there's a personnel cutback at City Hall, we get policemen, firemen, and slow movers from the driver's license bureau."

As they crossed the concrete walk, Grover pointed out that there was cement everywhere. This was, as he had mentioned to his bosses many times, very bad for hooved animals. The cheery animal keeper then stopped to admire the view they had of the river. It was high today, Grover noticed. There had been a lot of rain and snow this winter, followed by hot days that melted the stuff into dirty slush.

"What happens to the zookeepers they replace?" Marcella asked.

"They're history," Grover replied. "Course, sooner or later, the feds pass some half-cocked crime bill which consists of giving the town enough money to hire the same guys back as cops."

"And then in two years it starts all over again," Marcella pointed out.

Grover continued, "We have a half-dozen exotic environment buildings here. We used to call them cages." Pointing to the buildings arranged in a half circle around them, Grover announced, "In the last few years, we've had massive renovations in our effort to transform this joint from a zoo into a wildlife habitat park. Those massive renovations consist of taking down all the signs that used to say 'Cat

House' and 'Bear Cages' and 'Zoo Cafeteria' and putting up signs that say instead 'Cat Habitat' and 'Bear Outdoor Environment' and 'Wildlife Habitat Park Cafeteria.' You see"—Grover pointed to the handful of guests trudging around the zoo—"how those changes have electrified the general public."

"Now, now," Marcella admonished, secretly enjoying the animal keeper's cynicism.

Grover led her over to a cracked and barren concrete pool. "This is the manatee pool. It's been empty for a good long time."

"Why's that?"

"People used to throw them coins and stuff, to see them dive for 'em," Grover shrugged.

"Jeez," Marcella responded, seeing where that was going.

"Yeah," Grover confirmed. "Killed them both. You're here long enough, you see the people who bring in boat horns to see how high the fallow deer will jump when they scare them . . ."

As Grover talked, he picked up a discarded fast-food bag and started filling it with the other garbage that had been tossed into the empty tank. "The people who throw the bears apples with razor blades inside. The little kids who throw rocks at the lions and leopards. The jerks who give monkeys glass bottles of juice or iced tea, which they break and then cut themselves with, all of these clowns, and then you think to yourself . . . maybe not all the animals are on the other side of the bars."

CHAPTER 4

While Marcella toured the Palmer Wildlife Habitat Park, Jackie faced the zoo that constituted her Friday class.

The problem with the film lab was that many students, athletes in particular, took the course as an easy Humanities elective. Having no real appreciation for films, and coming from a culture where films were trouble-free moving pictures to be burped at and commented aloud upon, their relationship to moving celluloid was not the same as in the case of the serious film students. Therefore, Jackie went back to the very beginning of her film material and started to talk about King Vidor.

"King Vidor was born one hundred years ago today, students. He spent three quarters of a century directing films. Let's take a look at the one thought to be his masterpiece . . ."

"Excuse me, Jackie!"

The dark-haired film instructor turned to see Dean Vingori, an instructor in the Music Department, standing in the doorway.

Picking her way carefully down the center aisle of the auditorium, Jackie fluffed up the sides of her hair and asked, "Did you need to talk to me?"

"It's your dog," Dean answered apologetically.

"Oh, yes?" Jackie was momentarily confused. "Jake? What about him?"

"He's outside," Vingori responded. "Barking up a storm. I think he wants to talk to you."

"I wonder what he wants," Jackie said, perplexed.

Vingori shrugged and went back to his office.

Jackie opened the door of the projection booth and stepped inside. What a thing to come up in the middle of her film lab!

Plucking her red wool flannel jacket off the coatrack, Jackie then addressed the bald, brooding projectionist, Dusty Lang, currently perusing a comic book. "Dusty, I have to run an errand. Do me a favor. Call my T.A., Arne Hyverson, and say I've been called away and we'll go over the film when we meet next Friday. See you later."

"Yeah," Dusty said, without looking up. "*Hasta la vista*, baby."

Jackie left the projector room, checked herself out briefly in the reflective glass of one of the hall corridor display cases, and saw that her ensemble— a black cotton polo shirt with a matching cashmere skirt, stockings, and pumps—was hanging together all right. She then rushed out the front door of the Longacre Center and located Jake, standing expectantly just outside.

"Jake!" Jackie called out, shivering. It was another cold spring day. "What's the matter, boy? Why didn't you come in?"

Jake looked at the handicapped entrance, which consisted of a ramp and a push-panel electronically opening door, and shook his head. Jackie walked over and pushed the low panel and saw that sure enough the door wasn't working.

"Well, that's too bad," Jackie said at once. "I'd better call Security and see if someone can come fix that."

Never mind that, Jake seemed to bark at her. *Come with me.*

Jackie looked around worriedly. "Is something wrong? Do I have time to get my bag?"

Jake shook his head impatiently and started down the sidewalk to the parking lot.

"All right," she said, and followed.

CHAPTER 5

While Palmer's premier amateur sleuth and her trusty canine sidekick headed for the Rodgers faculty parking lot, Marcella's favorite pet, the largest two-year-old puppy anyone had ever seen, a bull elephant mastiff named Maury, worried the chain that held him not very securely to a BICYCLES ONLY sign on the edge of the Palmer Wildlife Habitat parking lot.

His beloved mistress, what's-her-name, had fastened him securely to the signpost just out of the reach of the row of parked motorcycles, bicycles, and a moped. Marcella hadn't counted on the fact that Maury had learned a great trick from his great pal Jake—who Maury considered to be something of a mentor. Maury's wise old pal had taught him to flex his neck muscles when the spike collar was put on and then to relax them later so he could slip right out.

Now, free as a bird, Maury was checking out the big Honda Road Hog parked first in line.

Maury liked motorcycles. The oil was like Chanel

27

to his highly sensitive nose, and the smell of the
seat—particularly when the rider wore leather pants
as this one apparently did—was sheer nirvana.

So impressed was the massive puppy by this piece
of machinery that he decided to pay it the ultimate
compliment. Unfortunately, in raising his leg, he accidentally nudged the protruding tank and the bike
promptly fell over. In going down, it hit the next
two-wheeled vehicle in line, a costly Italian racing
bike. The bike dominoed into the next bike and
then the next and the next until in a matter of sec-
onds the entire line of bikes was toppled.

Jeez, what a mess! Maury thought to himself. *Somebody should clean that up.* Then, with a final sniff or
two at the air to see in which direction his food-
providing mistress had gone, Maury set off to do
some damage somewhere else.

Marcella, meanwhile, continued her grand tour with
the whistle-blowing animal tender, Grover Gilmore.
They had just reached the Aviary-Simian House, a
crescent-shaped building with outdoor cages on
both sides.

Inside, there was a pedestrian walkway that separated the monkey cages from the bird cages. A narrow alley, behind a three-foot wall, ran alongside the
cages that separated them from the walkway. A long
radiator ran underneath the wall. A cleaning hose
was wrapped around a section of the radiator that
had never worked. Four drains, one every ten feet
or so, were embedded in the concrete of the alleyway's floor.

"This," Grover said, introducing Marcella to the birds, "is the new animal tender, lords and ladies . . ."

The birds, dressed in their feathered finery, looking like hangers-on in the court of some corrupt medieval king, came to look at the interloper. Some of the male birds immediately preened and displayed their fan feathers. The female birds clucked in disapproval, and scolded or made lewd gestures in their newest competitor's direction.

"Most of our collections come from the Gulf Coast of the United States and Mexico. We have mangrove cuckoos, great white herons, Florida Key flamingos, and toucans from the Yucatán peninsula," Grover related. "Out in the man-made marsh down to the left there, the wading birds hang out when it's warmer. The ducks and geese are hiding, but you'll see them if you toss some fresh fish into their lily ponds." As Grover strode down the alleyway, he pulled out a stout wooden feed box.

"Are those boxes locked?" Marcella asked.

"Usually," Grover answered. "Unless the last person forgets. They're all different locks, but every full-time animal tender has a master key which opens all of them. If we decide you need one, I'll get a copy of mine made for you. The keys aren't anything special. You can get one made in any hardware store."

As Grover tossed handfuls of seed up into the birds' feeding trays, he continued to introduce the cast of avian characters. "If you'll look up to the second row of cages up there, you'll see jewel-throat warblers and cockade woodpeckers. Over there are roseate terns, brown noddies, and blue-faced boobies, who are real pirates. You have to keep them from stealing everyone else's food.

"Out in the salt ponds, by the artificial marsh, we've got plovers, sandpipers, sanderlings, assorted gulls, royal terns, clapper rails, the short-legged or attenuated black-necked stilt, and the smooth-billed anni, which looks like a grackle in need of a nose job."

"What," Marcella asked, "is a grackle?"

"This is a grackle," Grover said, taking out a special dried plantain treat and holding it through the bars. "Susannah! Oh, Susannah! Won't you cry for me?"

The grackle, a strange marsh bird with the feathers of a cockatoo, the neck of a cartoon vulture, and the beak of a toucan, dropped down, looked Marcella full in the face, and yelled something that sounded like "What'll it be?"

Marcella laughed. "Not while I'm working, thanks." She then turned with amusement to Grover. "Did you teach her that?"

"No," the amiable animal tender smiled. "I can't take credit for that. They all say something like that. It's just that Susannah's call really sounds like she's a bartender greeting a bunch of vacationing traveling salesmen. Susannah, want a cracker?"

Marcella noticed that the cracker Grover was holding out to the bird was a dill-flavored wafer, a personal favorite. Why, if it weren't for the fact that who knows what animal had dragged its tongue across these crackers, she may have requested one herself.

"What's the matter, Susie?" the animal tender, obviously as pleased as punch to be performing for such a distinguished audience, asked. "You don't want this cracker?"

Susannah held her head in ninety-degree angles, first to one side, then to the other.

"Oh, I get it," Grover responded, pulling an aerosol can out from the box. "You do want this cracker, but you want it with cheese!"

Marcella chuckled as the animal tender sprayed cheese on the cracker in the shape of an "M."

"In honor of our distinguished visitor," Grover bowed in Marcella's direction.

The anchorwoman curtsied. "Thank you very much."

Snatching the cracker out of his hand with a head motion almost too fast to see, Susannah took it aloft.

"She acts as if she hasn't eaten for days," Marcella commented.

"Don't let 'em fool ya," Grover responded. "There's all sorts of hanging feeders up there. The cheese on a cracker thing is more than just food to a bird like Susie. It's a status thing. Grackles often hoard food, like a miser hoards money. Then it'll sit up on its perch and start yelling to other grackles about how much of a wad they have.

"After a coup like this, she'll probably break off a piece, wave it under her friends' noses to rub it in, then eat it right in front of them."

"Like she's got so much hoarded food, she can

afford to go ahead and eat a tasty morsel like this without sweating it," Marcella finished.

"Hey, you catch on fast!"

"You don't get glamorous jobs like mine if you're a slow reader." Marcella then adjusted her hated wig and wriggled her nose disgustedly. "What is that smell?"

"Just what you think it is," Grover answered smugly.

"I don't suppose the Palmer Parks Department ever considered investing in a few stick air fresheners?"

"We use every air freshener known to man in here, and it don't help a bit."

Marcella looked nervously skyward, reminding Grover of Tippi Hedren in *The Birds*, only brunette.

"We don't have to worry about . . . ?"

"Nah," Grover smiled again. "Their *kiosco* . . ."

"What's that?" Marcella asked quickly.

"It's a sort of gazebo bird sanctuary," Grover replied. "As you see, it doesn't extend over the walkway here. And gravity usually takes what they drop straight down."

"Usually?"

"Well, there's a joker in every crowd. These guys got a lot of time on their claws and sometimes they learn to shoot it out a little. How did you think I got all those streaks in my hair? I'm not that old, you know."

"Grover, really," Marcella responded.

"Oh, oh." Grover danced in place so delighted

was he. "Don't tell me I made the big TV anchorwoman blush."

"You're going to make the big TV anchorwoman
leave in a moment," Marcella replied. Then, realizing how harshly that had come out, Marcella soft-
ened her tone. "No offense, Grover, but I've got to
deliver five features a week—so I can't make this
story my life's work. Can we cut to the chase?"

"Sure, sure," responded the animal tender, a little hurt. "I'm not trying to bore the pants off you.
I just wanted..." Grover then broke off and
headed down the corridor.

"What?" Marcella called after him.

"Never mind," Grover replied, without turning
back.

Marcella, walking quickly, caught up to Grover before they went through the revolving door into the
Simian House and tugged on his sleeve. "Come on,
whatever it is, tell me."

"It's just that..."

"What?" Marcella asked, now genuinely curious.
"You can talk to me, Grover. I'm not going to laugh
at you, or get offended, or give you away, or whatever it is you're afraid of. You can tell me. What is
it?"

Grover shuffled uncomfortably from foot to foot.
"It's not that big a deal and now we've made such
a big thing about it, I'm uncomfortable telling you,
but..."

Marcella gave him an expectant look.

"I could just show you the lousy things..." Grover's voice caught as emotion overwhelmed him.

"The sick animals, we've got a hippo that's never really been well; the overweight, underexercised yaks and zebras; the babies, like the little possums who are born sickly and malnourished and die because they don't get their shots. I could tell you about the animals who got sick or died because the cage temperatures weren't high enough when it got cold, or because they were stomped to death in an overcrowded cage. And maybe you'd react to it, or maybe you wouldn't quite get it unless I explained it to you. Or maybe you wouldn't think it's that big a deal. I know you've covered a lot of fires, and child abuse things and car accidents and the whatnots. Maybe it doesn't affect you anymore . . ."

"It affects me," Marcella said earnestly. "It really affects me a lot sometimes, Grover."

The animal tender swallowed past the lump in his throat. "Well, I'm glad to hear that, Ms. Jacobs . . ."

"Carly, remember?"

Grover tried to smile, but the effect was pretty woebegone. "Carly, the thing is, it affects me too. More than most of the stuff that happens to humans, if you know what I mean. I live with these animals every day. They're like babies to me, you know? Or at least like patients in a hospital. I mean, I'm sorry it has to be like that. It's not a lot of laughs sometimes looking at these guys—like the leopards who like a lot of space and instead get a ten-by-ten with a tree that has one branch too fragile to hold any of them. Or the lions. Man, that's sad. In the grasslands they're kings and queens—here they live in a garage where the plaster falls from the ceiling on their heads when it rains.

"I mean, what kind of miserable monsters do they think we are, sometimes? I try not to think about that. I try to think of this place as a rest home, you know, for animals who need looking after. Animals don't like being cooped up like this. But let's face it. A lot of 'em couldn't really hack it on their own anymore. Especially poor Hokey the Elephant who's had two heart attacks and now is living on borrowed time. I try to deal with 'em on that level and it usually works, but it's tough, you know? To see one of these old guys go when I know we could have done something to help them."

Marcella nodded and reached for her notebook.

"You heard," Grover continued, "about the capuchin monkey—Lenny—who cut his foot on a piece of glass and bled to death. It happened at night. Nobody knew."

"That's terrible," Marcella said softly.

"Yeah, it sure is," Grover agreed. "I saw Lenny get born here. When his mom died of pneumonia, I bottle-fed him with my own hands and now they accuse me of hating monkeys."

Marcella looked up from her scribbling. "I'm not following."

Grover did not go back, instead going on to say, "I have begged the Parks Department for three years to put up a sign about it. I mean, not all of the people who give bottles of stuff to animals are sadistic. Most of 'em don't know any better. You just have to tell 'em that if they're going to give something to the animals to make sure it's unwrapped. If it's something to drink, all they have to do is put it in a paper cup or a juice carton.

"But no, they wouldn't spend the money. I put up a handmade sign, you know? It looked neat. It wasn't offensive. Then someone tore it down. I put up another one. The boss had it taken down too. He calls me in and tells me, I can't put any signs up unless they're officially sanctioned. Says it doesn't look good. Maybe it'll give people an idea that the other two monkeys who died the same way Lenny did should have been a warning to us. That Lenny's death could have been avoided. There'll be lawsuits, maybe. Then we'll all be out of a job."

"That's terrible," Marcella responded. "Who is the supervisor here?"

"Mort Slake," Grover responded. "Do you know him?"

Marcella answered in a troubled voice. "Yes, I do. I've had dealings with him when he was on the City Council and they weren't very pleasant, I can tell you."

"Yeah, well. I don't know how pleasant he is these days," Grover responded. "I don't spend that much time with him. But I know about animals and running a zoo, I beg your pardon, a wildlife habitat park, like this one here, and I know he's doing a lousy job."

"How exactly?" Marcella asked at once.

"That's what I want to show you, now," Grover replied. "This is the most unbelievable thing you've ever seen. I am now going to introduce you to the biggest human killer this or any zoo has ever seen."

Grover threw open the door and then, all of a sudden, before either could react, a blur of feathers and cartilage struck out.

"Aaagh!" Grover yelled.

"Oh!" Marcella fell back into the aviary, hitting the floor heavily, banging her elbows and the back of her head.

Grover screamed again.

Marcella then heard a sickening sound like a watermelon being dropped on a backyard patio, and then a thump, and then a loud bagpipelike victory cry.

This inflamed the other birds in the aviary. The air filled with "Don't peck me"'s and war cries, and feathers flew down from all directions.

Then suddenly an enormous nine-foot colossus—a big mad bird—the terror of the bird family, a bird capable of jumping five feet in the air and kicking through a brick wall, jumped into the doorway.

It was Beau, the wildlife habitat's not-so-captive ostrich, and he had blood lust in his eyes.

"Oh, my God!" Marcella said aloud, frantically trying to slide backward.

The outburst gave the behemoth a tracking beacon on her voice, and he hopped right toward her.

Marcella rolled to one side just as the ostrich's blunt beak, containing the strike force of a sledgehammer, smashed into the concrete floor, cracking it and sending chunks of cement flying.

Holy cow, Marcella thought to herself as she continued across the floor. Who booked her a room in this nightmare? Marcella then rolled until she was in the drainage ditch, slamming up against the cages.

The ostrich, listening carefully, hopped around on the other side of the room, looking left and right for his next victim.

Marcella flattened herself in the deep ditch, now very nearly below floor level. Unfortunately, the cages were right next to her and the birds, at last given this chance for petty peasant revenge against their masters, slammed into the bars in their haste to peck or scratch her with their razor-sharp claws.

Slapping at them with her left hand, Marcella reached up ahead of her with her right hand, pushing through the muck and stagnant water in the ditch until her hand clasped upon a rusty metal drain cover. Prying the heavy round piece of metal out of the drain with her now-broken fingernails, Marcella popped the piece of metal free and elevated her head until her eye was just above the level of the floor.

The ostrich, doing its distinctive war dance, was crowing again. The cries had the aviary in an uproar.

"Go, Beau!" they seemed to say.

Marcella felt like she was in the midst of the Roman Forum and that she and the bloodthirsty Beau were battling gladiators.

Waiting for the bird to avert his head for a moment, Marcella threw the drain cap near where Beau was standing, then dived toward the Simian House. For all Marcella knew, there was a seven-hundred-pound silverback ape in there, waiting to take his turn on the tag team of death, but the newswoman knew she had to do something if she did not want Beau to do a Mexican hat dance on her already-bruised body.

As Marcella made her dive, Beau launched himself for the place where she had lain just moments before. Hurtling through the doorway, Marcella crashed down next to poor Grover.

There was no blood, Marcella was glad to see, but the way his lifeless body flopped around as she searched for his keys, she could tell he was dead.

Suddenly Beau slapped into the doorway.

Marcella backed away on the floor, trying to con centrate as every rhesus, capuchin, white-face, chimpanzee, baboon, and medium-sized ape screamed, gibbered, hooted, and roared with lusty approval for the sort of life-and-death struggle that they and their jungle forebears used to witness constantly.

Seeing that there was no door out on this side of the building, Marcella edged toward the cages. Some of the monkeys immediately came to the bars to touch the pretty lady as she passed by. One or two pinched her. A jealous red-tailed baboon snatched her wig off and proceeded to chew on it. Brushing her hair out of her eyes, Marcella moved to the radiator.

Beau, bouncing on the heels of his claws like a fighter, bobbed over, strategically placing himself between Marcella and the only route to freedom.

Marcella then bent down to the radiator and started unwrapping the hose. Beau stalked the plucky newswoman and was just about to make his final death lunge when Marcella whipped the length of industrial cleaning hose around and caught the murderous bird on the side of the head with a heavy titanium nozzle.

Beau groaned and jumped backward. As he recovered and attacked the abandoned hose as if it were a snake, Marcella ran through the door back into the aviary.

The pandemonium was incredible. The birds had scented blood and now were howling for their share of the kill.

She heard heavy-footed plodding after her and knew that she would never be able to run the length of the habitat before Beau caught her. She dived for the first set of cages and reached it with moments to spare. Inserting Grover's master key, she managed to get herself inside, and the door closed, before Beau caught up.

This was not, Marcella reflected, as she slipped and slid backward, turning out to be a very good day.

CHAPTER 6

Blissfully unaware of the perilous fix his beloved mistress what's-her-name was in, Maury scampered along, browsing through the wildlife habitat smells the way an inveterate reader loves poring through stacks of books at a secondhand store.

When a cute boy came to pat the nice doggy, Maury cheerfully licked the lad silly, ate his hot dog, and then accidentally knocked him down a hill into an artfully sculptured bush.

Maury just loved kids.

When a security guard tried to eject the elephant mastiff, Maury played a brisk, invigorating game of tag, ending up by goosing the guard over a low fence into an interesting smelling pile of fertilizer.

Then he had a nice roll in the children's garden, flattening out each and every little popsicle stick with the individual children's names on them.

What a good day he was having!

All of a sudden, hearing the sound of his screaming mistress, Maury rushed off to do his famous doggy cavalry imitation. Maury loved to be the hero of the day. This, not the life of the average chained-to-the-tree yard dog, was the role Maury knew he was destined to play.

While Maury thundered to the rescue, Jackie Walsh, nudged and guided by her semipsychic dog Jake, raced across Palmer. Jake had communicated in no uncertain terms to Jackie that they had to get to their house at once.

"I hope," Jackie replied, wincing as they ran over a speed bump, "that this is worth missing *The Big Parade* for."

In the aviary of the Palmer Wildlife Habitat Park, Marcella continued her attempt to escape from the murderous feathered furies that surrounded her.

"Meow!" she yelled, unsuccessfully trying to imitate a cat. Then, remembering something her father, a Pennsylvania farmer, had taught her, Marcella held her arms out and whirled around and around. This worked just the way the scarecrow on their family farm had done, and the birds, unnerved and demoralized, left off their attack.

At the same time, Beau started kicking the bars of the cage. Marcella, knowing it would be only a matter of time before the long-legged battering ram smashed through the ancient rusty bars of the cage, started climbing up the side.

Boom! Boom! Boom!

Beau was nothing if not methodical.

Reaching a level of five feet off the ground, Marcella paused for a moment. The bars narrowed as she climbed higher, and Marcella found that she could no longer find purchase for her boots. This, unfortunately, was as far as she was going to go.

Seeing that his prey had stopped for a moment, Beau, down below, took a moment to catch his breath and to let his massive body pump blood back into his flat, mean little head.

Marcella noticed that the aviary was suddenly quiet. Had the vicious little turncoats grown hoarse from gloating over her imminent demise—or was this another tactic to unnerve her?

Deciding she would call their bluff, Marcella started yelling, "Help!" Beau, craning his head and twisting his mouth to show intense agitation, squawked angrily and rushed toward the door.

Blam! it flew open.

"Oh, no!" Marcella yelled. For the first time in a long time, she was genuinely scared. So frightened in fact was Marcella, that the news anchor used a magic phrase that had not crossed her lips since she was a schoolgirl. *"Please,"* she yelled frantically. "Help!"

CHAPTER 7

Jackie burst in through the front door.

"Peter!" she yelled.

Grabbing firmly on to the back of Jackie's jacket with his teeth, Jake kept his mistress from falling headlong over a hockey stick, a sack of pucks, and a hockey goalie's left leg pad. Jackie swore volubly and howled for her son's hide.

This was really too much! Peter wasn't a goalie— he had no reason to have a leg pad! Jackie's son was actually bringing home other kids' equipment to create a bigger mess for her to deal with!

As Jake frantically tried to soothe his mistress, Jackie climbed the stairs of her narrow, two-bedroom rental. "Peter!"

Using his mother's steam iron to melt a plastic gob off Captain Wight, his skeleton captain, Peter was deaf to his mother's cries. People had been yelling at Peter Walsh all his life and shouting didn't make him listen any more. It made him listen less. Peter had learned that lesson from TV, where the commercials were louder than the programs, so after a while you learned to tune them out.

"Peter!"

All of a sudden there was a slam and Peter's door flew open.

"Peter!" Jackie shouted. She hated shouting. It made her tender, expressive voice sound harsh. "Didn't you hear me calling you?"

Peter assumed a protective Ninja Turtle stance. "I thought we said you were going to knock before you came into my room?"

Jackie gave her son a look. "Do you really want to start a contest of who broke what promise?"

"Well," Peter grimaced. "It's okay that I don't keep my promises, because I'm under eighteen and most of the rules of the land don't apply to me. Because I'm an innocent youth, you know . . ." All this talking was distracting Peter from the task at hand and he burned Captain Wight's leg. Smuckers! Now he would have a pegleg captain. That would be weird. Peter immediately lost himself in reverie wondering whether or not a skeleton pirate captain could have a wooden leg.

"Peter!"

"What?!"

"Is that my iron?" Jackie demanded.

"Maybe," the young boy conceded. Here again he knew enough from watching those Perry Mason TV movies to admit to nothing that couldn't be proven in a court of law. Nowhere on the iron in question, Peter noticed, was there any sort of name tag identifying this particular steam iron as belonging to Jackie Walsh.

Steaming far more than her iron, Jackie snatched up the now plastic-encrusted appliance and yanked the cord out of the wall.

"You really should turn that off before you unplug it, Ma," Peter advised.

"Stifle!" Jackie shouted.

Peter, never having seen *All in the Family*, was baffled by the allusion.

"Why," Peter's mother went on to inquire loudly, "is there hockey equipment, let alone pads that you don't actually use, scattered all over my hallway?"

"It was wet," Peter improvised. "I didn't want to track up the house."

Even Jake rolled his eyes at this one.

"And the goalie leg pad?" Jackie demanded.

"Bobby Blue gave me that leg pad," Peter explained.

"Why?!" Jackie asked.

"Well, you know, it's got a few rips in the stuff . . ."

"Fibrafoam," Jackie supplied. She knew from dating a policeman in the past that bulletproof vests were filled with the same tough fibrous foam that lined football helmets and hockey leg pads.

"So I figured I'd patch it up and use it for something."

"Peter, darling," Jackie tried to control her impatience with the boy who had been such a delight for the first one and a half years of his life, "putting aside the question of how long it's going to take you to get off your dear little bottom and do something as ambitious as fixing something, what exactly did you think you were going to do with a leg pad?"

"I don't know," Peter admitted. "It didn't cost nothin'."

Jackie turned on the full heat lamp glare she had inherited from her mother.

"All right, all right," Peter conceded. Then with the air of a millionaire dismissing a servant, he allowed, "You may dispose of it."

This was too much for Jackie. She reached out, grabbed Peter's ear, and demanded, "Honey! Was there perhaps a phone message for me today?"

"I don't know," Peter whined. "You're hurting me. I'm going to call a lawyer!"

"What's this?" Jackie asked, pointing to Peter's arm.

"Oh, yeah. Marcella called."

"Peter . . ."

"Ow!" Peter cried. "You're going to make me look like Mr. Spock."

"Just on one side, dear," Jackie pointed out reasonably. "Let me change sides."

"Ow!" Peter yelled again as his mother switched ears.

"I want you," Jackie instructed her troublesome adolescent boy, "to leave phone messages for me on the pad downstairs, or on a piece of paper where I can easily find it," Jackie instructed. "Understand?"

"Anything, anything," Peter groaned.

"I'm serious, Peter," Jackie concluded, releasing her son.

"Oh!" Peter collapsed onto the bed and tried

hard to work up a sob. Unfortunately, the feeling of a pillow against the boy's slightly fuzzy cheek had the usual effect and in a few moments he was drifting to sleep.

Mistress and dog exchanged disgusted looks. Jackie picked up a black marker and wrote on the unconscious boy's arm, "Honey, I'm going to see what Marcella wants. Be good! See you later."

Boom!

Marcella torqued her body to the left, avoiding the first hopping strike by the murderous ostrich.

She flipped around so she faced the ostrich and nimbly baby-stepped to the right to avoid the next attack.

Suddenly, seeing the birds snickering down at her from their perches above, Marcella had an idea. Trusting her instincts, she launched herself through the air and grabbed a hanging bird feeder.

As Beau, below, looked on perplexed, Marcella trapeezed to the other side of the cage.

It was the damnedest thing he'd ever seen. What kind of sick, crazy psycho would play around with the food provider and spill the seed and suet that was supposed to last him and his buddies all winter, just horsing around?!

Hopping over to line her up for a death blow, Beau was stunned as she did it again, swinging back to where she had started from!

It was raining bird food now, and all the others were starting to get unnerved as well.

Birds aren't really picky eaters, you see. They're

just used to surviving tough winters where they have to make a certain amount of food last a long time.

Beau hopped to the other side, genuinely scared now. Marcella was not aware of this, but Beau's fellow birds were starting to turn on him—to scold him for upsetting their food arrangements. Who was going to refill their half-empty feeders now? Surely not the animal tender he had just killed.

All of a sudden, the door to the aviary swung open and Hoss Greenaway appeared, carrying a shovel. "I'll save you, Carly!" he yelled in what he considered to be a heroic voice.

Beau turned to the fresh meat with a malevolent smirk on his horny little beak. So the man wanted to play, did he? What could be better? This would afford him a graceful out for leaving the woman where she was. Then, once he killed the little fat boy, Beau would be able to escape and wreak havoc across the countryside.

"Don't worry, Carly!" Hoss cried again.

Marcella, watching closely as Beau hopped out into the corridor, gingerly climbed down from her perch. She feared that the monster bird would make short work of the former pizza delivery boy.

However, Hoss Greenaway surprised both beauty and beast. Choking up on the shovel as if he were trying to hit a ground ball to drive in a run, Hoss attacked Beau, bruising one leg and knocking the ostrich sideways. Beau regrouped and jumped up in the air, kicking like Bruce Lee. This mighty kick, powerful enough to separate Hoss's head from his shoulders, missed connecting by inches.

Hoss ducked, showing surprisingly swift reflexes, and brought his shovel up halfway. Beau then feinted and struck out with his strong rudimentary wings.

Hoss took the elbow without falling, but his guard dropped enough to allow Beau a clear shot at the shovel. In a moment the ostrich had yanked the shovel out of his hands and had smashed it against the bars.

As the metal plate and thick wood handle fell to the floor, Marcella yelled, "Run, you idiot!"

Hoss did not take the suggestion. Instead he stood transfixed, looking over Beau's shoulder at the newswoman who now stood in front of him in the corridor, waiting to make her sprint for freedom.

"Why, Carly," Hoss stammered, struck nearly dumb by her newly revealed blond locks. "You're beautiful."

At that moment, Beau struck out with his beak, grazing Hoss on the left side, breaking two ribs. Pumped with adrenaline and barely feeling the pain, Hoss absorbed the blow and was able to pull himself up for another round.

Beau, a little surprised, struck out first his left wing, then his right, backhanding Hoss to the floor and then breaking the boy's flailing right wrist. As the young carrot soda heir started to choke out something about "Don't worry, Carly, I have matters under control," Beau kicked him once, twice, three times, breaking the boy's legs, bruising his ample buttocks, and giving Hoss a concussion the likes of which had not been seen since football players had played without helmets.

Beau then contemptuously hopped over the broken but still alive Hoss and swaggered for the door with much the same attitude that Jack Palance had exhibited after gunning down the poor sap farmer in *Shane*.

There was, however, one more obstacle for the bloodthirsty ostrich, namely one big dog named Maury.

"Arf?" he asked cheerfully. Here's where his mistress had gone! What a nice place! Birds and everything. Boy, a guy could do worse than retire to a place like this when he got a little older. Between the animals and the friendly park patrons and the interestingly odored animal tenders, a dog could keep busy.

Giving Maury a superior sneer, Beau reached out, as if brushing aside a young fan asking for autographs, and slammed his left wing against the dog's left shoulder. It should have collapsed him like a balsa wood house, but Maury just grinned at Beau. The blow stung a little, but he didn't care. This was great! The big goofy bird wanted to play Hit Shoulder! Why he hadn't played that since he was a pup! Maury loved Hit Shoulder!

Maury then took his turn, roundhousing Beau with a big meaty right paw, sending the two-legged terror rolling like a big white tumbleweed toward the cages.

The birds were stunned. They had never seen their champion go down. Why, when Beau and his late wife Sadie had been released from the container trunk in which they had been shipped across the mighty Atlantic, it had taken six burly teamster types with sticks, nets, and tranquilizer darts to wrestle the monsters into their cage.

Squawking that he was all right, but taking a nine count, Beau jumped to his feet. Beau was actually a little surprised at how woozy he felt. He responded with a halfhearted kick.

Dodging the leg easily, Maury opened his mighty jaws, caught the bird by the ankle, and then joyously started running to Marcella as if bringing his mistress a stick.

Was there any better dog in the world?

At the same time, in the late Grover Gilmore's locker where Marcella had stored her things, a cellular phone started to ring. It was her good friend Jackie Walsh, returning her call.

CHAPTER 8

"This is hilarious," Marcella commented the next day, referring to the tall blue glass vase of dyed silver and white ostrich feathers that Jackie had brought in lieu of orchids.

"Hey, it's cheaper than flowers," she cracked. Sitting down in an orange visitor's chair, Jackie asked more seriously, "How are you feeling?"

"Much better now," Marcella smiled, fastening the top buttons of her pale green nightgown, "after receiving the capable ministrations of the Marx-Wheeler staff."

Suddenly Kevin Erlanger, Marcella's boyfriend and the fellow in charge of the Medical Center's TV rental franchise, emerged from the bathroom. Jackie could immediately guess at the sort of therapy Marcella had been receiving. She nodded at him in greeting.

Marcella continued, "I still cough up a feather every once in a while, but other than that I'm okay. What about my good friend Beau the limping ostrich?"

"Still at large," Jackie replied.

The phone rang and Marcella quickly picked up. "Yeah? Put him on." She then turned to her guests and mouthed, "Stan Gray."

"How have you been, Jackie?" Erlanger asked.

"Fine, fine," she replied. "And Maury is his usual rambunctious self."

"I really appreciate you taking him for a while," Erlanger said with great sincerity. "Just until Marcy's back home. With the hours I put in here, Maury would be alone most of the day and I shudder to think what might happen."

Jackie nodded her head in sympathetic understanding. Maury, who had let Beau make his escape when the big dog became distracted by a piece of chewing gum stuck on the floor, could be a force of great destruction. Even under watchful scrutiny, Maury had the same effect on private property as a Texas tornado.

"Well," she replied, "I guess we can't neglect the hero dog."

Marcella, still holding the phone to her ear, made a face and used the remote control to turn on the big twenty-five-inch TV Erlanger had brought up for her.

The voice of KCIN-TV anchorperson Drew Feigl filled the room in all its slightly nasal New York glory. "This is Drew Feigl . . ." It was said that the lanky, dark-complected newsman was the object of passion among Palmer's news-watching female viewers, but Jackie, for one, could not see the attraction.

Now, Kevin Erlanger, on the other hand . . .

"I am coming to you live"—Feigl raised an eyebrow—"from the Palmer Wildlife Habitat Park, once known as the Palmer Zoo. Yesterday, the calm little environment was turned upside down when Beau, the ostrich . . ."

A stock picture of a mean, beady-eyed ostrich flashed on the screen.

". . . husband of the late Sadie . . ."

A stock picture of the same ostrich, but shot at a different angle, was flashed on the screen. ". . . went berserk."

A picture of Morton Slake, a sturdily built man in his early fifties, with thick, wavy brown hair, flashed on the screen.

"Morton Slake," Feigl continued, in voice-over, "acting supervisor of the Palmer Wildlife Habitat Park, said he didn't know who was responsible, but someone managed to sneak past the crack Habitat Park security staff and entered the Aviary-Simian House . . ."

A distant shot of the Aviary-Simian House was flashed on-screen, with inset icons in the corner representing a monkey and a parrot.

Drew Feigl then resumed on-screen, ". . . and slew poor Sadie with some sort of blunt object, while Beau was in another cage, helpless. Apparently, after the ostrich's mate had been murdered, the killer . . ."

Kevin Erlanger looked at his watch. "I really should be getting back, Marcella . . ."

"Just a minute, Kev," Marcella pleaded. "It'll be over in a minute or two."

The three continued to watch as the news program aired a clumsy "dramatic reenactment" of the incident that had Jackie's eyes rolling.

Finally, the image changed to an unflattering still of Horace "Hoss" Greenaway, III, and Drew Feigl's voice took over the narration.

"We'll have more later on the vicious attack and attempted murder of popular Palmer handler, Horace Greenaway, and the savage killing . . ."

Jackie thought it odd that young Hoss Greenaway's injuries, severe as they were, would be given top billing over the murder of the man who actually was the Palmer Wildlife Habitat Park's most popular animal handler, but then remembered how much the McKean Beverages Company advertised on the station.

". . . of Grover Gilmore, another employee at the park."

Erlanger kissed his lover on the forehead and moved for the door. "I've got to split, hon. Feel better."

"I already do," Marcella smiled. She turned off the television with the remote control.

"I better go too," Jackie said, rising. "I'm playing poker tonight and I've got to find some way to restrain Maury while I'm out."

"You're a doll, Jackie," Marcella said with apparent sincerity, giving Jackie's hand a grateful little squeeze.

"You bet your . . ." Marcella's phone drowned her out with a sudden ring. "In fact," Jackie continued, "when you get out of here, you owe me big time!"

Marcella, smiling, answered the phone. "Hello? Yes, Stan. I saw it."

Jackie wiggled her fingers good-bye and exited into the corridor.

"All right, that works," Marcella was saying as Jackie walked away. "Cut from the 'man being hit by lightning' segment to the sports and have Palooka Joe or whatever his name is start his segment with: 'And speaking of which, Palmer fans were electrified by J. A. Ditko's broken field running . . .' "

As Jackie walked to the window to see if she could see her Jeep in the south parking lot, she couldn't help but overhear a conversation between two people standing waiting for the elevator. Carmen McGowan, a surgical scrub nurse whom Jackie remembered from other visits to the hospital, was berating a well-dressed hospital administrator whose face Jackie could not see from her angle.

"Dick," the nurse was saying, "this isn't fair to me. I have needs too, you know?"

"Please, my dear," the administrator sneered. Jackie could see now that it was Dr. Richard Bellamy, Marx-Wheeler's chief administrator. "Let us not descend to schoolyard name-calling. You never hinted that I did not 'fill your needs' before."

"I'm not talking about sex, Richard," Carmen McGowan said angrily, her voice rising. "I'm talking about wanting to have some security. I love you, Dick. I want to have your baby . . ."

Bellamy half turned, saw that Jackie was nearby and listening, then grabbed Carmen McGowan's arm and squeezed tightly. "Must we discuss this matter in front of half the hospital?"

"Ow, you're hurting me," Carmen McGowan cried out, pulling her arm loose. "And if we can't talk now, when can we talk?"

"Later on," he responded.

"Where?" Carmen McGowan demanded. "You're not coming over to my apartment again until we work this thing out."

"All right then," the hard-drinking physician said through clenched teeth. "At the other place then . . ."

"You mean the . . . ?"

All of a sudden the bell for the elevator rang and a split second later the doors opened to release a herd of noisy neurologists. Jackie did not hear the rest of what Bellamy and the nurse were saying.

It was none of her business, Jackie chastised herself. She reached into her shoulder bag, pulled out a cellular phone, and coded in the numbers she needed to dial up her mother. Craning her head again, she tried to locate her Jeep. The last time she had gone off and left Maury in the vehicle, he had managed to overturn it, denting nearly every part of the car big enough to hold a dent. This time she had left Jake in the car as well, to calm Maury down, but she was still worried. Maury had a disconcerting habit of destroying something so fast that even the most vigilant human or dog was powerless to stop him.

Worried, she turned her attention to the ringing phone. Hmm. Jackie wondered why her mother wasn't picking up. Frances Costello had said she would be home all afternoon. Maybe she should stop by later on, after she visited Hoss Greenaway.

Ringing for the elevator that the administrator and his paramour had just disappeared down, Jackie decided to try once more, just in case. This time her mother answered on the second ring. "Great day in the afternoon," she said cheerily.

"Hello, Mother," Jackie said, smiling. It was good to hear her mother sounding so hale and hearty. A short, spry woman with a peaches and cream complexion and a beautiful nimbus of snowy white hair, Frances Costello was generally pretty healthy, but she had been laid low by a bad case of the flu for most of the winter.

"So . . . you're still seeing the actor?" Frances asked with a casualness so contrived as to be ridiculous.

"Yes, Mother," Jackie answered tersely. It never took long until Frances started interrogating, criticizing, or otherwise driving her daughter crazy.

"It's been what—a year now?"

"Something like that." Jackie's words were now so clipped that she was afraid her lipstick would chip and fall off in neat little slices.

"Well, then," Frances continued, ignoring her daughter's warning tone. "I suppose we'll be hearing the lovely peal of wedding bells anytime now?"

"No, Mother. That's the elevator bell you're hearing. Hold on, please." Jackie switched her phone to

Pause and boarded the elevator. She was about to pound something in frustration when her eyes alit on Nancy Gordon, the Hispanic ex-wife of Palmer's medical examiner, Cosmo Gordon.

Anger turned to pleasure and the two women embraced. "Nancy," Jackie said with pleasure. "What are you doing here?"

"This is one of my volunteer days," Nancy reminded her. "How about you? You're not sick?"

"No, no," Jackie responded as the elevator slowly ground its way down to the main lobby. "I was visiting Marcella."

"Oh, dear," Nancy unconsciously crossed herself. "I heard about what happened on the radio."

Jackie nodded sympathetically. The local TV news had become such a joke, people who really wanted to know what happened in the world listened to radio, just as they had in Jackie's mother's day.

"She's feeling much better," Jackie informed the former beauty queen, whose teenage daughter, Katharina-Elena, was a very talented concert pianist.

"Good," Nancy commented. "I feel so bad for poor Grover though."

"How did you know him?" Jackie asked.

"Such a lovely man," Nancy said, smiling with wistful memory. "Cosmo and I were on the board of the zoo for many years. We would be invited to all the special events—mostly so we could contribute money . . ."

Jackie knew that Nancy had some family money, but she was unclear as to how much, exactly.

"I became fairly friendly with Grover. He was the

sweetest man. And when he told me of some of the things that had gone on in that horrible place . . ."

"Which you and Cosmo did everything you could to take action on, I assume." Jackie wasn't being sarcastic. During their marriage the Gordons had donated most of their time to worthy causes.

"No," Nancy said sadly. "Regretfully, when my marriage ended, so did my access to the board."

"Hmm, that's interesting," Jackie said. "So . . . how are you really? Has it been hard on you?"

"What?" Nancy asked. "My divorce from Cosmo? What can I say? It came through last month. I've decided that I'm going to start dating again. I haven't done it for twenty years, but it's got to be like riding a bike, right?"

Jackie raised one eyebrow. The elevator touched down and Jackie and Nancy emerged into the cheap red plastic decorated lobby. "Listen . . ."

"Yes, dear?"

"Would you like to come over to my mother's house tonight and play poker?"

"Me?" The medical examiner's former wife was taken aback. "Really?"

Jackie squeezed Nancy's hand. "I'd love to have you come, Nancy. And if you play, you'd be doing us a favor. Half the regular group can't make it tonight, and we need at least five players to make a game."

"Well, I'd love to come. What can I bring?"

"Just a moment," Jackie replied. The two women stopped near a pillar festooned with plastic boxes of pamphlets. The pamphlets pretended to be on topics of general health interest, but they were really cleverly disguised come-ons for high-priced medical procedures and costly clinics. Nancy browsed through one which asked on the front in lurid red twenty-five-point type, "Does Cable TV Cause Glaucoma?" while Jackie took her mother off Pause.

"Hi, Mom," Jackie said.

"Is that you, dear child?" Frances asked weakly. "Oh, praise be to the Lord, Jacqueline Shannon. At my age, you know, you never can tell from one moment to the next which breath might be your last. Of course, if my dear only child sees fit to have me hanging on the phone the length of the afternoon, I'd never complain. Even with these shooting pains I get in me leg."

"Mother, I'm very sorry," Jackie said sincerely. "You know how these elevators are in the hospital."

"Well, I know that they're run by a lot of wee hamsters in the basement running around on a lot of cheap plastic wheels all day, if that's what you're asking," Frances responded. "Now, are you coming to poker or are you not?"

"I'm coming, Mother."

"Good. That's two of us. Marj might show up, too. And Bara will make it—if that new boyfriend of hers will let her out of the bedroom."

"And Jean Scott is coming, of course," Jackie contributed.

Frances sighed heavily. "Aye, I suppose the old bat will drag her bag of bones over here."

Jackie laughed. Jean Scott, the book reviewer for the *Chronicle*, was once a rival for her father's affections. She and Frances had been friends ever since, but not close friends.

"All right, Mother," Jackie said. "That's four definites. We need at least five, so I'm bringing Nancy Gordon . . . Cosmo Gordon's ex-wife, Mother. No, I think she understands that there won't be any husbands there for her to steal," Jackie then turned to her friend. "Do you want to come anyway, Nancy?"

"What the heck," Nancy said in the same spirit.

"Yes, Mother. She'll bring forty dollars. No, Mother. I'm sure she's good for it. Of course I understand, Mother, that you'd rather not take a check . . . until you know her better. I'm sure it's the same the whole world over. Just one thing. Nancy wants to know if there's anything she can bring."

Nancy stuffed the brochure she'd been reading back in its slot and prepared to pay attention. It was now her mission in life to get something—whatever it was that this crabby woman wanted—and to make it so big and so expensive and so excessive that Jackie's mother's mouth would fall open. And when her jaw did drop, Nancy would shove this something, whatever it was, right down her throat.

"What's that, Mother?" Jackie listened, looked guiltily at Nancy, and then switched the phone to her more distant ear.

"Why, yes she is, Mother." Jackie nervously played with her hair. Some women did this, Jackie had read somewhere, to show they were attracted to a man. Jackie did it whenever her mother made an embarrassing remark. People were always complimenting Jackie on her lovely curly hair. Jackie had given up explaining long ago that her hair would be as straight as Joni Mitchell's if it weren't for her dear, slightly bigoted mother.

"Yes, Mother. I'll be sure to tell her. You get some rest now. Good-bye."

Nancy turned to Jackie. "What are you supposed to tell me?"

"Nothing," Jackie mumbled.

"Come on . . ."

"She said," Jackie responded, "don't bring flan."

CHAPTER 9

Maury was pathetically grateful to see Jackie, his beloved former mistress, and this nice-smelling lady friend of hers. He restrained himself, with the help of an occasional reminder nip from Jake, until Jackie and Nancy were seated in the front seats of the Jeep. Then, while the two women were reaching for their shoulder harnesses, Maury reared up, put a mighty paw on each woman's shoulder, and drew them together, causing their heads to crack together like coconuts, for a big group hug.

After explaining to Maury that what he did was wrong, Jackie took two aspirin and dropped Nancy off at her own house. Hopefully, the ex-beauty queen's double vision would clear up before the poker game.

Jackie then drove to the next stop on her list and fastened Maury securely to a stately oak at the base of the driveway. "Stay!" Jackie ordered. Maury hunkered down like the good dog that he was, and immediately fell asleep and dreamed he was just one

of a pack of wild, rabid dogs, terrorizing the Maine
countryside.

Jackie and Jake then set off for the Greenaway
Mansion on the hill. "Greenaway" was not an os-
tentatious affair. It just stood out in the fashionable
Marland Heights area, where everyone had money,
because there were not many antebellum fieldstone
mansions north of the Mason-Dixon line. Jackie
knocked on the door.

A tough-looking woman opened the door. She
had purplish hair, a deep voice, and went by the
name of the month she had been born in. "April?"
Jackie asked.

The housekeeper gave Jackie a nod so brief she
may have imagined it.

"I spoke to you on the phone. I'm Jackie Walsh.
I'd like to see Horace Greenaway, Junior."

Jackie didn't know that Hoss was actually Horace
Greenaway the Third, so the dark-haired film instructor was a little surprised when she was ushered
right into the parlor, where Max Greenaway and his
lovely wife Phyllis were entertaining a few friends.
Collectively, they were known as the Palmer
Group—some of the most important men and
women in the entire city.

In addition to the burly Max Greenaway, who
looked like Wallace Beery with lighter hair or Ernest
Borgnine with a lantern jaw, and the imperial, aris-
tocratically thin Phyllis Greenaway, who snorted and
talked through her nose like Lily Tomlin's Ernestine
character, there were also the Dills—elderly brothers whose extensive business holdings included the

company that manufactured Peter Walsh's Teen Skater skeleton figurines.

Jackie also recognized one of the world's worst bosses, former gimmick store owner and current newspaper baron, Sam Sharpe. Sharpe was a big, bald man who consciously modeled himself after the Ian Fleming villain Auric Goldfinger. He was sitting next to Liz Curtis, Phyllis's sister and the co-owner of the McKean Beverages concern. A not so gay divorcee, Liz, despite her unending efforts to look young with all sorts of plastic surgery, hair color treatments, and stringent fitness regimes, now looked like Phyllis's mother.

"What's this all about?" Jackie wondered. And then, as if answering her question, Jake snatched a folded 4 x 6 card from an end table. Jackie, pulling it from his jaws, opened it and read quickly: "1. Palmer Zoo 2. Mall Financing 3. Reelection Fund." Glancing at the upper left-hand corner, she saw the word "Agenda."

"I believe that's my note you have there," a strident voice called out. It was Jane Bellamy, the dragon lady mayor of Palmer, who sported a black cigarette holder straight out of a Joan Crawford film.

Before Jackie could respond, Max Greenaway bellowed, "Well, look who's here. Great. You're just in time."

Jackie found this remark a little strange. Was the former police commissioner perhaps mistaking her for someone else?

"Pull up a chair," Max commanded. "We're

about to see the new commercial for McKean Beverages.''

''Watch your back, Max,'' Jane Bellamy advised as Max sat down next to her.

Max Greenaway then pointed a remote-control device as big as a brick and the Greenaways' giant seventy-two-inch monitor lit up. He pointed again and his videocassette player started to run the uncut version of the new commercial that would air during the broadcast of the next Palmer Panthers football game.

Afterward, the group applauded politely. Greenaway waved away the applause that he clearly felt was his due, then announced, ''My dear wife suggested I should get a couple of ex-cops to break Goodwillie's legs''—Greenaway referred to the cagey old local millionaire who had quickly cashed in on the European bottled water craze, becoming one of the first and biggest domestic bottled water manufacturers in the United States—''for getting into the beverage business in competition with us . . .''

''Now, Max,'' Phyllis protested, mostly for form. ''You know you shouldn't discuss our bedroom talk in front of strangers.''

''What are you talking about, honeylamb?'' Greenaway demanded. ''These people aren't strangers.''

''That person''—Liz Curtis pointed a bony, jewelbedecked finger at Jackie—''is a stranger.''

''And a busybody,'' Bill Curtis announced. The former mayor of Palmer, ex-husband of Elizabeth McKean Curtis, and Palmer Group legal adviser—

who had been in the bathroom until now—spoke up. "Watch her, Max. She's probably investigating the zookeeper killing. Give her half a chance and she'll find a way to tie you into this."

"As a matter of fact," Jackie said, nodding toward the agenda pages on the table, "I see that your little group here is having some kind of discussion about the zoo. You know, there are rumors flying that you guys have plans for it. I think the most recent story I've heard says you want to replace it with a Teen Skater theme park."

"What's wrong with that?" Pete Dill asked at once. For a moment it looked as if he was going to invade Jackie's personal space, but a low growl from Jake soon disabused him of that notion.

"I don't know that there is anything wrong with that," Jackie commented. "I think Teen Skater is sort of goofy . . ."

"Ms. Walsh here is a screenwriter," Jane Bellamy informed the others—having ferreted the information out of a hand-held computer notebook that had recently replaced her familiar deck of rubber-band-held cards.

For many years the former urban planning professor at Rodgers University had kept files on many of the prominent citizens of Palmer—particularly those with any influence on other voters. Jackie had once been fairly friendly with Jane, although she always found the woman more than a little bit weird. Jackie had been very sympathetic to the problems Jane Bellamy had undergone with her philandering husband, since Jackie's own ex-husband Cooper had suffered from the same weaknesses. However, Jackie did not appreciate the fact that once Jane Bellamy had succeeded Bill Curtis as mayor, she had continued to run City Hall in much the same corrupt manner.

Each time they had come up against each other in the last two years, as Jackie investigated, in her own casual way, several murders that had involved the mayor in some peripheral way, their relationship had deteriorated further.

"I am not actively pursuing my screenwriting career," Jackie defended herself, "and I have never worked in animation or resented or envied anyone who did. My only point is that the Wildlife Habitat Park is a cheap, quiet, and pleasant place for parents to take their children . . ."

"Woof!" Jake protested.

". . . and pets," Jackie added. "And if you want to close a place like that in favor of some high-priced tourist attraction"—Jackie rose to her feet—"you're going to get some opposition from the people here in town."

"We can allow pets . . ." Pete Dill started to offer.

"I'm afraid that's against the law, Peter," Jane Bellamy snapped.

"Everything's against one law or another," Dill said dismissively. "Surely people can buy indulgences, the way sinners were once able to buy forgiveness in advance from the medieval church."

Such erudition was lost on Max Greenaway, who responded by drawing upon the knowledge of police procedures he had acquired during his days as

Palmer police commissioner. "Don't worry, people. The police have better things to do than hassle law-abiding citizens out stretching their legs with their faithful pets . . . and I guarantee you," he continued, "that the Teen Skater Park will be user-friendly for people . . . and for animals too."

Phyllis Greenaway snorted once to get everyone's attention, then turned to Jackie. "Now, Ms. . . . whatever your name is. What do you want from us, exactly? Shall I have my housekeeper bring me a checkbook? Is that what it's going to take?"

"I don't want your money," Jackie answered, getting to her feet. "And I'm not investigating the murder of Grover Gilmore . . ."

"I believe the newspapers are calling it an accident, Ms. Walsh," Sam Sharpe rumbled.

"Well, you own most of the newspapers, Mr. Sharpe," Jackie pointed out. "So you should know. I'm here to pay a courtesy visit to your son, on behalf of Marcella Jacobs, who is still in the hospital. Beyond that, I didn't know Mr. Gilmore. I also don't know what's happening with the Wildlife Habitat Park and I don't have any particular expertise on animal behavior."

"Wonderful," Sam Sharpe said at once. "We'll take that as a commitment then."

Jackie smiled her famous crooked smile. "You wish." She then carefully slipped one of the agendas into her bag and explained, "I have, however, helped the police solve several cases . . ."

"Woof!"

". . . With Jake's help," Jackie quickly added.

"Enough to say this." Jackie addressed the whole group. "I would advise you all to come clean now. If the police or news reporters have to leave their comfortable chairs and tramp around in the cold and snow and actually do a lot of hard work ferreting out stuff, they're going to resent you. And anything they come up with will probably be blown out of proportion to look a lot worse than it actually is."

"I'm sure everyone here appreciates your advice, Miz Walsh," Frank Dill responded in his dry wheezing voice. "But as Mr. Sharpe pointed out a few moments ago, this unfortunate affair was, after all, an accident."

"It was made to look like an accident, I guess," Jackie allowed.

Jake could barely suppress a snicker.

"But someone killed Sadie," Jackie pointed out. "Then that same person let Beau out of his cage. Perhaps that person didn't know that Grover Gilmore would run afoul of him . . ."

"Oh, brother!" Bill Curtis complained.

"I think though," Jackie, who had not intended the pun, continued, "that the police are going to want to know who did it. If any of it can be traced back to any of you, let alone all of you, it's going to be heap bad publicity for Teen Skater."

Jake nudged his mistress and pointed his snout at Bill Curtis, who was recording what Jackie was saying with a small cassette recorder.

She nodded. "Are you getting all this, Bill?"

"Every word," the tall former mayor answered confidently. "It's like we used to say in Wyoming, ah'm just giving you enough rope to hang yourself."

"Save a good stretch for yourself," Jackie advised. "Anyway, you all may get your Teen Skater Park even with the bad publicity, even though one person died and two other people were seriously injured . . ."

"Ms. Jacobs was seriously injured?" Sam Sharpe interrupted. This was distressing news to the corpulent media baron. He had always had a sneaking attraction to the blond TV newswoman.

"Not at all," Jane Bellamy said at once, brushing ash off her black silk Chinese pajamas. "According to Dick, she has nothing more than a few superficial bruises and lacerations."

Jackie turned to Jane with a beautiful smile. "Why, Jane—*superficial?* Marcella could have a concussion or whiplash problem that won't manifest itself for a few days or even weeks. You of all people should know that."

Jane winced. She knew that Jackie referred to a spurious accident she had had on a city bus, which had led to a lawsuit that eventually netted her enough money to run for mayor.

"The fact of the matter is," Jackie continued, "it doesn't matter. Marcella is hurt and the moment she returns to the Evening News, even if she just has a bandage on her nose, she's going to get a lot of sympathy from her devoted fans."

This hit home with the Palmer Group. They all knew that what Jackie said was true. No one was better at pretending to be a warm, friendly, sympathetic

TV newsperson in all of Palmer than Marcella Jacobs.

"And Marcella is not going to forget this whole
incident in a hurry," Jackie continued. "She's not
happy that her first visit to the zoo, or whatever you
call it, was almost her last, and she's not about to
let another newsperson scoop her on her own story.
She'll want to know who set Beau free and why they
did it. And I suspect, no matter how long it takes,
that Marcella will find that out. So if you're involved,
you'd better be careful." Jackie was ready to let it
go at that, but as she moved to go up the stairs to
Hoss's room, Pete Dill ran over to her and grabbed
her arm.

"Jake."

Jake immediately got between Jackie and Sneaky
Pete and backed him off.

Almost hopping up and down in frustration at his
inability to put his hands on her, Pete Dill demanded, "What possible good could it do us to free
an ostrich and kill some poor animal handler and
rough up a newswoman and the son of our good
friend Max?"

"I don't know, Pete," Jackie said confidently.
"It's possible that whoever set Beau free didn't
know how much damage he would cause, but I
don't think that the person really cared."

"Posh and bother," Frank Dill wheezed, joining
his older brother in the hallway. "This is the sheer-
est speculation."

"Perhaps," Jackie responded, climbing the first
stair. "But I can defend it. Someone bludgeoned

Sadie to death. You don't have to be a Rhodes Scholar to figure that an act like that was going to anger Beau. Then that same person set Beau free, knowing that it was going to create a dangerous situation for anyone who might be in the path of that ostrich. Whoever did that, my friends, is in a lot of trouble. And if one of you put someone up to that, then you're going to be in a lot of trouble too."

CHAPTER 10

Jackie went up to Hoss Greenaway's room. Apparently not in any great pain, Hoss was reclining in a king-size bed, playing a game on a computer that seemed only a little smaller than the one Matthew Broderick used to threaten the entire world with in *War Games*.

"Hi, Hoss," Jackie greeted the young man.

"Who are you?" Hoss asked. The young bottled soda heir had been looking at the screen for so long he had contracted a temporary case of an ocular condition very closely akin to snow blindness.

"I'm Jackie Walsh."

"Woof."

"And this is Jake. We met before. On the Rodgers campus. Remember?"

"Oh, yeah," Hoss recalled dimly. "You're the lawyer."

Jackie wondered at the allusion, then remembered that the last time she had seen the boy, he had been delivering pizza and she had successfully argued her way out of paying for the pile of pies

that Maury had consumed. "No, I'm just a film history instructor. I was sent by Marcella Jacobs."

"Oh, boy." He sat up immediately. "How is she?"

"Marcy's on the mend," Jackie answered non-
committally. "No broken bones, fortunately."

"More than I can say," Hoss pointed out.

"I am sorry," Jackie lied. It wasn't that she dis-
liked Hoss especially, but she considered working
with large animals to be the sort of thing that led
inevitably to broken bones, whether you were an al-
ligator wrestler, a bear balancer, a bronco buster, a
bull rider, or just the owner of a large clumsy dog
like Maury.

"Mind if I sit down?"

"Sure, plop down anywhere," Hoss said cordially.

Jackie sat on the bed, then bounced up and down,
uncomfortably. "My goodness, this is a hard mat-
tress."

"Actually, ma'am," the white-faced boy responded apologetically. "You're sitting on my leg
casts."

"Oh, dear," Jackie said, springing up. "Are you
all right?"

"Sure, sure," Hoss forced out through clenched
teeth. He then reached for a large bottle on the
nightstand. "It doesn't matter. The doc left me
plenty of pain pills."

"I am sorry," Jackie said, this time sincerely.

"My fault," the boy said bravely. "I should have
dragged myself to a better position. There's a chair
over there, if you want to haul it this way."

Jackie looked over to the cluttered desk and saw

a rolling chair, almost completely buried beneath young Hoss's soiled laundry. "That's all right," Jackie responded, knowing but not saying aloud that after several similar encounters in her own son's room, she had vowed to herself to never again disturb a mass of adolescent boy's clothing without rubber gloves and a large can of bug spray. "I can only stay a minute."

"Gosh, is this your dog? Hasn't he shrunk or something?"

"No, no," Jackie said distractedly, fishing through her bag for the "thank you" gift that Marcella had given her for Hoss. "That's Maury you're thinking of."

Jake immediately shushed Jackie.

"Oops."

"What's the matter?" Hoss asked.

"We try not to mention . . ." Jackie dropped her voice down to where it was practically a whisper, "Maury's name, if we can help it."

"Why not?" Hoss asked reasonably. "Where is he?"

"He's outside, tied to an oak tree," Jackie responded.

Hoss shook his battered head and laughed. "Then what possible difference could it make if we yell—*Maury!*"

Jackie and Jake gave each other looks and slowly shook their heads. In the distance a baying started, much like what the master sound mixers of Hollywood came up with for the various screen versions of Arthur Conan Doyle's *The Hound of the Baskervilles.*

Talking fast so she could get back to Maury before he made a break for it, Jackie asked, "Hoss, how long did you work for the Palmer Wildlife Habitat Park?"

"About three months," Hoss replied. "Remember that reporter guy?"

Jackie nodded, knowing that he referred to the *Chronicle*'s boneheaded cub reporter, Charles "Bingo" Allen. "Yes?"

"Well, he wrote that article," Hoss said, "on how the pizza company was hiring all the kids of the richest families in town, you know, in order to buy influence in City Hall."

"Right." Jackie noticed as she listened that Jake was laying his head on the bedroom floor, much the way Tonto used to do in the old *Lone Ranger* serials. This made her wonder how long the stout front door and crack household security staff would be able to hold back the intrepid puppy.

"Then my boss found out that I was the whistle-blower," Hoss lied, sipping milk from a blue plastic glass shaped like the head of Captain Kangaroo. "Even though, you know, I didn't really have a whistle. I mean, I hate to tell you this, but I can't even whistle through my lips, really. It just comes out like I'm breathing, you know, maybe with a little note here and there, but nothing good. You know, like the theme of the old *Andy Griffith* show?"

"Cut to the chase, Hoss," Jackie instructed, raising her voice over the thumping sound downstairs quite likely caused by a two-hundred-twenty-pound elephant mastiff pounding against a steel-reinforced door.

"Okay," Hoss agreed, "but don't worry. That door's plenty strong."

"So's Maury," Jackie replied.

"Anyway, the pizza people fired me. So Mr. Allen, well, ma'am, he got me a job at the Wildlife Habitat Park."

"Just like that?" Jackie asked.

"Well, I had to lie on my application form," Hoss admitted. "I told them I used to rustle cattle in Montana."

The thumping on the door stopped.

"But, Hoss," Jackie pointed out. "Everyone knows your family. Most people know you're just out of high school. Who would be fooled by lies about you being a cowboy in Montana?"

"Well, no one, I guess," Hoss admitted. "I had to contribute six hundred dollars to Mr. Slake's campaign fund."

"He isn't running for anything, is he?" Jackie asked.

"No," Hoss responded, reaching for the bent-metal hanger he kept by his bed for scratching down under his casts. "I guess he gets to keep this fund and all the money in it for six years, then he has to run for something else or come up with some other scam."

"Hmm," Jackie said to herself.

Jake then barked, calling attention to the sound of breaking glass.

"What the heck was that?" Hoss asked.

"Maury breaking a window," Jackie said, wincing. "Talk fast, Hoss. Tell me about Morton Slake."

"Not much to tell," Hoss replied. "He took my check, called the bank to see if it was good. Then he shook my hand and said, 'Welcome aboard.' "

"What kind of handshake does he have?" Jackie asked.

"Dead fish," Hoss replied.

Cries and squeals were wafting up the stairs. "And did you work with Grover Gilmore the whole time you worked at the Wildlife Habitat?" Jackie asked hurriedly over the racket.

"Pretty much."

"Why were Beau and Sadie in separate cages the day of the attack?" Jackie asked.

"Sadie was feeling poorly," Hoss replied. "Maybe it was something she ate. Ostriches will eat just about anything shiny—bottle caps, rocks, whatever. The vet was going to come to give her an abdominal CAT scan."

"They can do that, right on the premises?" Jackie asked.

"Sure," Hoss shrugged. "They got portable stuff now they developed to take X rays of football players, right down on the field. It's not the best, but it's good enough for ostriches, I guess. Especially if they swallowed something easy to see, like a lightbulb."

All of a sudden, the door burst open and Maury, dragging a broken leash behind him, barked a greeting that nearly deafened them both. Apparently someone had opened the front door to inves-

tigate the damage he'd caused, giving him the
opportunity to dart right in. Sniffing around for a
moment, Maury became fascinated with, and soon
began consuming, one of Hoss's cowboy boots.

"Hey," Hoss protested. "That's my new Frye
boot."

"Sorry. I'll send you a check," Jackie snapped.
"Look on the bright side—you won't be needing
boots for a while anyway."

Hoss looked down at his twin leg casts and
gulped, "I guess you're right." After a resigned
pause, he decided to change the subject. "What did
Marcella send me?"

"Why she gave you . . ." Jackie held out the gift-
wrapped box.

"Oh, boy," Hoss exclaimed, reaching out.

Jackie quickly snatched the present back just out
of Hoss's reach. "Just one more question."

"Ohh . . ." the injured teen whined. "What?
What do you want to ask me now?"

"Explain to me," Jackie demanded patiently,
"how the door locks on the cages work."

Hoss was reluctant to cooperate, but at the same
time anxious to show off all he knew. "They work
about the same way as any cage works. You put in a
key, or a master key, the locking bar slides back, and
the door opens out into the corridor. Some of the
new cages in the other houses slide to one side, and
I think there are a few that open electronically. I've
never actually used any of those."

"All right," Jackie replied, absorbing the information. "Now, Marcella said she opened the door

to the bird cage with a key in order to temporarily escape Beau.''

"Right.'' Hoss nodded as vigorously as his injuries would allow. "But Beau managed to kick the lock until it broke and he was inside the cage with Marcella until I managed to distract him into the corridor.''

Hoss's recounting of the story carried with it a bragging tone, but Jackie let it slide. If Hoss was perhaps taking a little more credit than he deserved, he had made up for it, it seemed, by taking a little worse beating than he probably deserved too.

"All right.'' Jackie moved on, while at the same time Maury moved on to one of Hoss's gym shoes. "But then I saw something on the news that the person who opened Sadie's cage to attack her, and then later opened Beau's cage so he could be set free, did it at a master panel out in back of the Simian House.''

"That's right,'' Hoss agreed. "Beau and Sadie, because they were so strong, were being kept in the unused indoor/outdoor gorilla cages on the simian side of the building. Since monkeys are so good at picking locks, none of these cages open from the corridor. You have to use the mechanical box outside.''

"So the person who opened the locks couldn't see which cages they were opening, from where they were standing?'' Jackie questioned.

"I don't think so,'' Hoss replied. "Course I never opened those cages. Only Grover or the other senior animal keepers would do that. It's tricky, you know, to know which cages to open and in what order. You have to make sure that every animal is out of the way when you do open them up so they don't get their paws or tails stuck in the slide mechanism, or so they don't run past you and escape."

"I imagine they have to be particularly careful with the ostriches," Jackie suggested.

"I guess," Hoss responded. "Hey!" he yelped, his attention swinging to Maury.

Jackie turned to see that Maury was now investigating a ship in the bottle model that Hoss had spent endless hours building.

"Careful with that!"

Maury, hearing himself addressed, turned happily to the bedridden boy, accidentally knocking the pricey model to the floor with his tail.

"Oh, no!" Hoss yelled.

"Sorry, I'll send you a check," Jackie recited.

All of a sudden Maury ran to the bed. He brought the upper half of his mighty body thumping down on Hoss's chest (knocking the breath out of him in the process) and started licking stray cookie crumbs off of his face.

"Help!" Hoss sputtered, as if going down for the third time.

"Stop, Maury," Jackie suggested, knowing that her words would not reach the big dog until, of his own volition, he decided to move on to something else.

"Hoss, I'm going to leave you this present from Marcella." Jackie tucked the wrapped gift under the boy's blanket.

"Ow! Ow!"

"I hope you feel better," Jackie concluded, signaling Jake to start herding Maury toward the door.
"I'm sure Marcella will get in touch when you're
both feeling better. I put my business card under
the ribbon on your gift. I'll be out of town, but I'll
be carrying my cellular phone with me, so just dial
the out-of-town area code first, then you can reach
me anytime, anywhere, if you think of anything that
might help catch the person who did this terrible
thing."

"You're not with the police," Hoss pointed out
sullenly. He had been licked silly.

"No," Jackie conceded. "But I know most of the
Homicide investigators and it might be easier for
you to tell me some little tidbit than to go through
all the formality of setting up an appointment with
the police to pass it on to them. They can get kind
of busy sometimes and forget to be patient and
grateful for information that a witness might only
recall after they've been interviewed. Or when you
want to tell them something that's . . . well that isn't
in a format they readily understand."

Jackie referred to her own experiences with the
Palmer police, who had occasionally blown her off
for sharing with them a rumor or an intuition or
perhaps an insight offered by a trusty animal companion such as Jake simply because this kind of information was not as easy to catalogue or present in
court as a fingerprint or a revolver with an easily
identified spent shell still in the chamber.

"Okay," Hoss responded.

Jackie led her dogs between the glowering house staff and out to the end of the drive, looking back over her shoulder and saying, for the third time in an hour, "Sorry. I'll send you a check."

CHAPTER 11

The poker game had started when John Peter Costello, Jackie's father, was still alive. He and his friends would play cards for nickel and dime stakes, drink, smoke odiferous cigars, and swap stories, lies, and secondhand anecdotes on every subject imaginable.

Frances had asked her retired husband several times to be included in these poker parties. She dimly remembered bridge parties they had gone to as a young couple when they lived in southern California. Although neither of Jackie's parents much liked the game or found their casual, inattentive style of playing to be in great demand, Frances remembered them as being a lot more fun than sitting around the house all the time waiting for her husband to unlock the door of his writing studio.

Pete Costello flatly denied his wife the opportunity to join him. This was the only time anymore that he and his aging, fat, and balding cronies got to discuss their desires for various women, local and famous (and all distinctly out of reach), and he would not give up these pleasant fantasy sessions for anyone.

Frances therefore had organized, mostly as a joke, a poker party of her own, comprised of the "playing card widows"—the wives of the fellows with whom Pete played poker. When Pete and his pals—Frances had lured them back to her house with a promise of homemade ice cream with pralines—had walked in, they had come upon the spectacle of their wives, seated at the round dining-room table, wearing eyeshades. Best of all, the women were seated under a large picture depicting dogs playing poker, and were pretending to spit, smoke cigars, and drink giant foamy mugs of keg beer.

The men had laughed like loons and had sat down to their bowls of ice cream, convinced that there was no way in heck that this group of women would ever come together and play poker in a regular orderly fashion the way they had done for some dozen years.

Frances and her friends, who originally had possessed no intention of carrying the gag beyond the evening, took this kidding as an affront and therefore decided informally to meet every other Thursday night, the same as the men. They weren't, at that point, really planning to make the poker game an institution, but Frances and her friends were determined to show their deadbeat husbands that they could be equally stubborn.

At first, in order to hold on to the nonpoker players, the Thursday meetings featured other card games besides poker, board games, particularly

Scrabble, and a general party atmosphere that allowed women to spend the entire night in the kitchen or in the living room cooking, knitting, or just visiting.

Eventually the nonpoker players drifted away and Frances replaced the original players with other neighbors, friends, and friends of friends brought in by the other poker members.

The game had hung on to this day. Meetings had been canceled no more than a half-dozen times in the ensuing years, and for all but a month or two when Peter Costello, in the last throes of the illness that eventually killed him, was home and needed full-time care, they had been held in Frances's apartment.

Jackie had joined the group as a pinch fill-in while still in her early teens and had kept with it for nearly twenty years, coming whenever she possibly could. Like most of the women, Jackie enjoyed the evening away from her lovers and family. The small stakes poker game—mostly between players who had been sitting across the table from each other for years and intimately knew each other's habits—did not take a lot of active concentration. This allowed all concerned the opportunity to drink, gossip, and work out for themselves problems which they had not been able to solve at home.

While Jackie did not necessarily unburden herself of every problem or concern at the regular poker parties, due in no small part to the fact that her mother was one of the players, she had found the women a responsive and stimulating audience when she was actively writing screenplays and wanted to discuss some aspect of the current project.

During the last days of her marriage, when Jackie and her husband Cooper had been going through some perfunctory relationship counseling, Jackie had found the characterizations offered by her poker group to be far more perceptive and to the point than the psychobabble chatter of the professional marriage counselors.

As Jackie arrived for the evening, letting herself into the apartment she had grown up in with her own key, she heard her mother saying to Bara Day, "Well now, there's nothing wrong with moving in with a fella before accepting his ring and tying yourself to him like a couple of brood mules harnessed next to each other pulling a beer truck, in my opinion. I'd a said different twenty years ago . . ."

"And in fact you did say different twenty years ago, when I came home and told you I was thinking of doing just that with Cooper," Jackie pointed out. "In fact, you told me that if I did any such thing, you'd drug my drink, shave my head, and ship me off to Israel to work on a kibbutz. Hello, everyone."

"Hey, babe." Bara Day was newly brown-haired—it had been snowy white until she met one of Jackie's associates in the Communications Studies Department, an elderly bachelor whose looks were as close as Palmer came to Douglas Fairbanks, Jr. The glint in her eye also told Jackie that things were going well.

"How's tricks, Bara?" Jackie asked.

"Couldn't be better."

"Hello, Jacqueline," Jean Scott, the very proper white-haired reviewer, seated directly across from her old rival Frances Costello, greeted her.

"Hello, Jean," Jackie said at once, taking her companion's heavy bags from her. "Do you know Nancy Gordon?"

"Sure I do," Jean answered affably. "You're Cosmo Gordon's wife."

"Not anymore," Nancy said brittlely. "And I hope when we take a break you'll tell me how I can put a personal ad in your newspaper."

"Why sure," Jean said at once. She didn't like to admit it, but she was a little taken aback. Jean herself had not had a date in the past eight years and had spent many a night bitterly weeping about her plight. It had never occurred to her, however, to actually do anything about it.

"Good news, all!" Jackie announced. "Nancy's brought something sweet to have with coffee later."

"Really?" Marj Leaming, the former City Council member, commented delightedly. Like so many recently retired seniors, the former councilwoman had decided to let her waistline go a little.

"Oh, just a few things," Nancy said lightly, removing her coat and negligently tossing it on the sofa. "I believe there are some *mamalitas* there."

"What's that?" Marj asked at once, feeling her round tummy growl beneath the folds of her pretty Elizabeth Ashley print.

"It's a Mexican dessert. I hope you don't mind some Hispanic delicacies?"

"No, not at all," both Marj and Jean Scott said quickly.

"*Mamalitas,*" Nancy explained, making sure her fellow poker players got a full view of her clinging black Norma Kamali original, "are little flour and sweet milk tortillas cut to two-inch lengths and rolled around a generous serving of rich pineapple and coconut custard."

The women flushed and grew involuntarily faint with arousal.

"We also have *crepes cajetas,*" Nancy continued cheerfully, "which are very thin pancakes rolled around a nut filling and covered with caramel sauce; chilled nougat with honey; mango which I will flambee with a tamarind/tequila liquor, pumpkin seed marzipan, and a Cointreau mousse large enough so that everyone can have plenty of helpings and then take some home."

Puffing like an excursion camel, Jackie dropped the enormous bags of exotic treats into her mother's narrow, high-ceilinged kitchen.

Frances then turned to Nancy with a patronizing smile and said, "Oh, I wish I knew you were going to bring a dessert, dear. I wouldn't have bought that bag of chocolate chip cookies and spent so much time arranging them nicely on the plate there.

"Oh, well. We'll suffer through. No one said life was a cakewalk. Do you have that forty dollars cash currency me daughter told you to bring? Might as well get to it, if we don't want to be here until the morning."

• • •

At the same time, in the office of the Palmer Wildlife Habitat Park, Supervisor Morton Slake poured his guest another drink.

"Hey, go easy on the Irish whiskey," Slake's former college roommate protested.

The former City Council president brushed the objection aside with a wave of the hand. "Come, come, Corky. Since when did you ever go light on the applejack?"

The honorable Corcoran R. Dole struck an innocent pose and orated, "Ever since I became the city district attorney, Mort. You know that."

"Know it? Hell, I half financed it." Slake wiped his brow with a paper towel. He was sweating like the proverbial grizzly in the sauna bath.

"Now, Morton. Let's not be crass. There were a number of contributors to the 'Elect Dole Whether He Deserves It or Not Fund,' I'm happy to say. Your contribution was generous but no more substantial than many others."

Slake leaned his head forward and barked harshly, "And just who do you think twisted those other contributors' arms? Jane Bellamy?"

"No, no, Mort," Dole quickly conceded. He was trying to stay cool but his shaking hand betrayed him. "I know, of course, that there's no love lost between the mayor and myself but . . ."

"She didn't want you, Corky," Slake taunted his old friend. "I had to get Greenaway and that crowd to muzzle her. Then I had to get Sharpe and the other newspaper boys to go along. Do you think their endorsement came out of midair? That they helped out an obscure real estate lawyer, whose only claim to fame was handling the holdings of the Slake family, out of the goodness of their hearts?"

"No . . ." Corky said nervously, taking gulps of his drink now.

"These people contributed because I told them to contribute." Slake sniffled without blowing his nose, then went on, "I told them to contribute because I saw you as a man we could do business with. Now let's not pussyfoot around anymore, all right?"

Dole finished his drink and nervously ran one of his trademark lavender silk handkerchiefs across his lips. "I am not trying to be difficult, Mort. It's just that we are, after all, in a fairly public place."

"We're in a zoo, you moron." Slake automatically poured an extra dollop of Irish whiskey into each glass without bothering to clear it with his old roomie. "There's nobody here but you, me, the drunken security guard—who's probably passed out in the first-aid room as usual—and a bunch of stinking animals."

Dole wrinkled his nose. "They do stink, don't they?"

"Yeah, they sure do," Slake responded with a sardonic grin. "They stink to high heaven." He wiped his face and opened his white suit jacket to reveal a blue-striped shirt soaked through with perspiration. "Is it hot in here or what?" He got to his feet and moved over to the ancient window air conditioner.

"Actually, Mort, it's rather chilly in here," Corky protested in vain. His silk suits were not worn for their warming properties, and the blast of cold air nearly caused him to start shivering.

"I just don't know what it is with me," Slake grumbled, coughing lustily into a paper napkin which had come with his lunch. "Must be coming down with the flu, along with everything else."

"Well." Dole grasped desperately for this opening. "If you're not feeling well, this is the last place to be—this drafty old cow barn."

"Damn it!" Slake exploded. "To hell with the smell and the draft, and the fact that you have to sit on a goddamn folding chair, Dole! You've had to put up with it for ten minutes. I've had to endure it for two years!"

"Don't try to pin this on me, Mort," Corky Dole snapped. He then stood up and reached for his coat. If nothing else, the district attorney thought to himself, if he did have to stay here and listen to the sleazy political hack who had once been his best friend in the world, he would be warmer. "I had nothing to do with you taking this job. If you'll recall, I was the one who told you that you didn't have to take another job right away. That even with the unfortunate settlement you got from your wife . . ."

Corky referred to Marie Zug, the eccentric Palmer designer who had divorced Slake after a scandal resulted from one of his many extramarital affairs.

". . . You still have enough income from your real estate holdings to live comfortably until your pension comes through." Morton Slake, like many politicians who had resigned from the public eye under a cloud of disgrace, had succeeded in keeping his swollen pension.

"I can't just sit around, Corky," Slake rasped.

Dole noticed that his old friend's skin was pale and clammy and that his palms were so wet that the former City Council president had to continually blot them with a paper napkin.

"And my expenses are a lot higher than you might think. I've been living in an apartment for the last year. Eating out all the time. No one to take care of my clothes. This job doesn't come with a car. You know? My credit's still shot—so I'm taking car services everywhere. I want to buy a house in the U district. I've got my eye on a place . . ."

"I understand. You've got problems."

Slake sneezed violently. "Problems? Yeah. I got a few problems. You want to see my biggest problem? Follow me."

In point of fact Corky Dole did not want to see Mort Slake's problem, but the district attorney sighed and followed him out into the corridor.

The floors creaked and groaned as the two men trod them, and the dim fluorescent fixture that provided the only light in the corridor flickered and seemed to reveal ghostly figures flitting by.

Mort Slake's office, once you stepped inside and shut the door, looked respectable enough—especially decorated as it was with furniture he had brought with him from the office of the City Council president. However, the moment one stepped out into the corridor, one was sharply reminded that most of the buildings that housed the Palmer Wildlife Habitat were once, in the not-very-distant past, dairy barns.

"I didn't remember," Dole mused as Slake, making unpleasant throat-clearing noises, locked his office door with his master key, "that cows smelled quite so bad."

"It wasn't cows that used to be here, Dole," Slake growled painfully through a raw throat. "It was goats. Milk goats. Damn idiots were convinced the goat milk industry would boom after a few health nuts started advocating the stuff. They lost their shirts."

"What happened to the goats?" Dole asked.

"What do you think happened?" Slake responded derisively. "They ate them. Makes a great filler in meat loaf. During the fifties half the meat you got in diner meat loafs was goat."

"Wonderful," Dole commented, putting up his umbrella as they walked outdoors.

They emerged on the unlit strip of asphalt used by the Parks Department as an access road, which separated the Administration Building from the main animal buildings. As they walked up the slight incline, Dole saw a couple up on the Cedar Lane overpass, lit by the one streetlight in the area. Clearly they were arguing about something. Scattered words floated down with the drizzle and the mist.

"This isn't fair, Dick."

"Why can't we just call it quits?"

"I covered up for you when we were lovers. What makes you think I'll keep covering your . . . ?"

"Hey!" Slake yelled up to them. Obviously he had not recognized the couple as Corky had done. Either that or the Wildlife Habitat supervisor simply did not care. "Hey! You up there! Take it somewhere else! You're disturbing the animals!"

Not bothering to see whether the couple was following his orders, Slake stumbled up the steep gravel ramp and Corky had to scramble just to keep up with him.

"Jeez, Mort," he complained. "Slow down, will you? I'm not wearing mountain-climbing gear, if you don't mind."

Slake didn't answer. Instead, he led District Attorney Dole to the now notorious Aviary-Simian House and around to the back.

"Mort," Dole protested at once. "If you are trying to show me anything to do with the ongoing investigation into the Grover Gilmore death, I have to excuse myself right now."

"This has nothing to do with ostriches, Dole," Slake responded with some disdain. "Just hold your horses. Hear me out and I'll walk you to your car."

Wheezing and coughing, Slake led the way, past the silent indoor/outdoor cages of the great apes and the empty cells that once held two four-hundred-pound ostriches.

"I want to introduce you," Slake said, "to the real troublemaker of Palmer Wildlife Habitat Park." Coughing again, Morton Slake pulled back a heavy blue rubber shower curtain to reveal the youngest monkey in the park.

"Gooey!" Corky Dole, like so many Palmerites, had closely followed the birth story of the little monkey and had cried like a baby when Jethrine,

Gooey's mother, had died shortly after the birth of her child.

"What's wrong with Gooey?" Dole asked worriedly.

"He's—" Slake started coughing uncontrollably. "He..."

Dole moved to his old employer and managed to catch the stocky man before he hit the ground. As he adjusted his grip and looked around for somewhere to lay the sick man, Dole noticed that Slake's right sleeve, which he had been using to wipe his mouth, was dark with blood.

"Check the ... House ..." Slake muttered. He then started to turn purple in the face and his tongue lolled out of his mouth.

Gooey, the cute little childlike monkey, reached out a tentative paw to his master as if to try to help.

Dole dragged Slake to the still-open back door and then, ignoring the shrieks and chattering coming from the occupants of the Simian House—who by now had a very low opinion of these frail, puny humans who regularly keeled over and had to be removed from their domicile on a stretcher—called out into the night.

"Doctor! Is there a doctor here?! The head of the zoo needs attention!" Dole then looked down at the desperately ill man, turning a dark purple color, and wondered if he did die, lying there on a straw-and offal-covered floor, whether there would be an investigation. If so, would it involve him?

Would someone somehow see something sinister in this after-hours meeting and blame him? Would this bring out the strange web of alliances which had brought him into office? Would this somehow be tied into the deaths two years ago that had cost Morton Slake, Mayor Bill Curtis, and Commissioner of Police Max Greenaway their jobs? Was this to be the end of Corcoran Dole's promising political career? Was this the end of everything? How could this happen to the Palmer golden boy whose life had never quite gone the way he dreamed? Would this final indignity break up his engagement to the beautiful Tracy, whom he had pursued for so long?

By the time Dick Bellamy, red-faced and wheezing, finally reached the stricken man, he had to push aside the maudlin lawyer who was lost in a miasma of self-pity. "Well, what are you waiting for, man?"

Dole looked up and focused. "Oh, Dr. Bellamy. It's you."

"Yes, it's me," Bellamy growled. "You're lucky I just happened to be in the area, er, walking my dog. Now I'll do what I can for this man. Get an ambulance down here right away."

CHAPTER 12

After a half hour or so of play it was as if Nancy Gordon had been a member of the poker group all her life.

"Hey," she said to Jean Scott, who had been helping her concoct a personal ad. "This is the fourth time you had me redo this ad. Why can't I say, 'I'm the catch of the year'? I *am* the . . ."

"I don't doubt that you are, dear," Jean responded, calling the bet and raising it a penny. "But this is not a beauty contest."

"Hey!" Nancy bristled. She understood that her beauty-queen past just made some women jealous, but although she had kept her expressive eyes and most of her figure, it wasn't as if she were still a beauty-contest winner today. It did irk Nancy that no one—not one woman she had met in the eighteen years she had lived in Palmer—had one pleasant thing to say about the fact that she had once been Miss Puerto Rico.

Perhaps an elderly woman who didn't even work in the classified section, for goodness' sake, couldn't imagine why it might be important to mention that she had a beauty queen's gold crown on top of her bureau, but Nancy more than suspected that this wouldn't turn any normal red-blooded man off.

"Dear," Jean Scott explained patiently, "a personal ad is not a shout—it's a whisper. It is as if you are raising your voice slightly at a party, telling your friend something that you want a man who interests you across the room to overhear. Would you tell someone you just met at a party that you are a great catch?"

"I don't know," Nancy considered. "I might."

"Well, you might tell the right man. Someone you've been talking to and who you think is enough on your wavelength to pass that kind of test, but not just anyone." Jean followed the betting, considered her cards carefully, and decided to risk the three cents in raises that had come up since her last go round. "An ad like the one you've just written will attract men, but the right man? I don't know. I should think you would get a lot of braggarts and phonies."

Nancy puzzled over the question, while at the same time trying to remember if Marj Leaming had taken two cards or three. "I suppose you're right. I call."

Marj folded her cards. "It's yours."

"Aha," Nancy grinned. "You were just bluffing a barefoot sugarcane girl, hunh?"

"That's what you should use," Jean Scott advised. " 'Barefoot sugarcane gal, all grown up and looking for the man who can court the woman but still see the pretty girl inside.' "

"You know," Nancy Gordon decided. "That's not half bad."

"Glad to be of help, dear," Jean responded smugly.

"But I still want to mention my beauty-contest titles!"

Before another argument could ensue, Jackie interrupted, "Speaking of men, Nancy . . ."

"Oh, me head," Frances exclaimed. "The topic has switched around to men now, has it? I suppose the only five minutes of the evening that were devoted to another topic besides men and food I just missed because I was washing me hands."

"The man I was going to ask you about," Jackie surged on determinedly, "was Grover Gilmore. You said you knew him?"

"He was such a nice man." Nancy smiled in memory. "Kind, warm, sensitive, honest, funny . . ."

"Too bad he's dead," Bara Day commented. "You could have married him."

"A zookeeper?" Nancy said, aghast. "Never!"

Little rodents, Maury thought to himself. *Is there any small creature more fun to stalk, destroy, and then devour? No siree, Bob.* The freely associated thoughts flashed into the mighty dog's brain like highway signs entering the peripheral vision of a speeding trucker.

As Maury thought to himself, he watched a sneaky skulking little cat stalk the mouse in the tenant's vegetable garden. *What a guy*, he thought to himself.

Maury admired cats. He thought it was cute the way they were always licking themselves to remove their scent so big dogs like him couldn't track them. Didn't work worth a darn though.

Still, you had to hand it to cats. They put in a good night's work, torturing mice, trying to find where sleeping birds were hiding, overturning people's garbage cans, ripping carefully planted greenery to shreds.

Cats are tough too, Maury mused. He would never forget the time he grabbed that calico cat by the tail and the little son of a gun clawed him right across his mighty nose. What a horrible act of violence that had been. His nose had hurt so much his beloved mistress had to get him an expensive shot of something at the Pet Pals Hospital. And it had ruined everything for him.

For weeks Maury was not able to smell properly. Who knows how many dogs had invaded his turf, left sneering messages for him on his favorite spruce tree, then walked away again, free as you please, without him knowing about it?

How many rabid squirrels had run up and down practically right in front of him without him knowing a thing about it?

And his food! Why without his nose to help him, the stuff tasted exactly like horse meat, cereal, and ash—and surely his beloved mistress would not serve him such garbage.

Maury then laughed again as the cat ran into an aluminum garbage shaft on the side of the building, knocking himself silly. Clumsy goof. No wonder cats did all their frolicking at night, proud, haughty little furballs that they were—they couldn't stand to be seen looking foolish.

Cats were not really great mousers, Maury reflected to himself. He, on the other hand, was a truly great mouser.

Maury would never forget the time he had followed his natural instincts and had placed a black wharf rat he had found by the docks on his beloved mistress's silk pillow. What lusty cries of delight she had given him! What loving cuffs with a slipper she had administered, killing in the process those pesky fleas that he could never reach.

What a great mistress! Was it any wonder why he loved her more than any mistress in the world? *Good old what's-her-name!* Maury decided right there that he would go look up what's-her-name this very evening and give her a tongue kissing that she would remember sitting in her rocking chair in the retirement home.

Getting to his feet, Maury grr'd a warning to the miserable cat who was still trying to focus his eyes after the knock on the head he had taken. Maury filled his chest with air, straining the shoulder harness that his temporary mistress Jackie has put on him to its limits. Maury then decided to tell the world that he was alive, awake, and spoiling for trouble.

"Orrooo!" Maury uttered. "ORROOO! *ORROOO!* ORROOO!"

In a moment, every window facing the courtyard opened. As the neighbors yelled their happy hellos

and shouted their bravos for his singing, Maury lustily gave his admirers a second chorus.

"ORROOO! *ORROOO!* ORROOO!"

In the apartment, Bara Day was telling the other
players a story about her boyfriend, Cyril Plumb,
when they heard the noise from the courtyard.

"What on earth is that?" Nancy asked, immediately grabbing her jewelry.

"If it were the war," said Marj Leaming, who had
been born in London, "I'd say let's go down to the
bomb shelters until the jerries are through."

"That's not a 'jerry' you're hearing," Jackie said
at once. "That's a Maury. Mother, does the window
in your bedroom face the courtyard?"

"No, dear. It still faces the apartment building
across Grant Avenue, just the way it did when you
lived here with your father and me for the first fifteen years of your life."

"Where did you go when you were fifteen?"
Nancy asked.

"I ran away to join the circus," Jackie answered
as she paced back and forth trying to think of some
way she could call Maury's name. Once she did,
Jackie knew, Maury would come running and the
noise in the courtyard would stop.

The howling grew so fearsome that the women
moved their drinks closer to the center of the table.
Jackie headed for the door.

CHAPTER 13

Dancing around on his back legs, his front paws held high like Rocky Balboa, Maury kicked the now useless harness aside and bellowed like a moose. The cat, still dizzy, felt his way toward the nearest tree.

Madder than they had been since the early days of the Roosevelt administration, the irate seniors who lived in the apartment complex heaved everything they could lay their hands on at the hell hound outside.

Donna Lee Botz, sleeping with her boyfriend Bingo Allen, the way she always did when her husband was away for the evening, looked up at the racket, and then saw to her consternation and horror that her digital clock had chosen that particular moment to malfunction and so read "666." Therefore the barking in her courtyard was obviously the beast predicted by Revelations!

"*Aaaaagh!*" Donna Lee screamed.

Bingo leapt up from his pillow to exclaim, "What the hell is going on?"

"This is it, Bingo!" Donna Lee wept uncontrollably. "Judgment Day!"

Frances and the others heard Jackie's voice from somewhere down below. "Maury! Maury!"

"Oh, the Good Lord preserve us. I don't even want to think of what will happen to me beautiful apartment when that waltzing bear of hers gets here." Shuddering, Frances reached for the pitcher of pink sloe gin fizzes and poured herself a stiff one. "Why she has to bring her two dogs with her, I'll never know."

"I don't see what you're complaining about," Jean Scott pointed out. "You have two snakes in your husband's old study, don't you?"

"Well, there she goes again," Frances said loudly. "I know I've said this many times to you, Jean Scott, but I'll say it again, if I must. Only one of the fourteen-foot pythons in the 'Snake Room' is mine. The other is Bara's snake, as you should well know. If your memory's that bad, dear, perhaps you should take to writing things down. Sensible things, not a few half-baked opinions on a bunch of low books that no decent person would want to read in the first place."

Jean turned pink to the back of her neck and it was clear if there'd been a half a grapefruit on the table she would have mashed it in her old rival's face with the same ferocity Jimmy Cagney had exhibited toward Mae Clarke. Instead, she spat out, "Well, now, Frances. That's a very challenging statement indeed, coming as it does from a woman who's never used a book for anything but killing a fly."

"There's more than bugs that can be swatted with a book, Jean Scott," Frances muttered.

Bara Day then gave Frances a disapproving kick under the table.

"I don't understand," Nancy Gordon said at once. "Why do you have these big snakes? As watch-dogs?"

"That's right, dear," Bara Day said at once. "They're the best burglar alarm you'll ever have. Bugs, mice, any kind of small animal, won't step over the doorstep. If a burglar sees one, he'll run through a wall like one of those Warner Brothers cartoon characters to avoid them. They're quiet. They're friendly. You feed them once a week. They don't need a cat box. You've got to pick up their old skin during the shedding season, but that's no hardship for such adorable pets," Frances added.

"When can we see these wonderful pets?" Nancy asked.

"Well." Bara was dubious.

"Hey," Marj Leaming said at once. "I'd love to get a look at them."

Frances at once staggered to her feet. She loved showing off her darlings. "Wonderful! You've called for a viewing and a viewing ye shall get. Right this way, ladies, to the greatest show on earth."

At the same time, down in the courtyard, Maury watched delightedly as a flying sneaker knocked the cat from his branch.

What a riot. People had been trying to hit yodel-ing, screeching, yowling cats for years without ever coming close. Now a shoe had actually found its mark, only because the owner was aiming at Maury instead.

A little bored from the cacophony, and a little thirsty after shouting himself dry, Maury ambled over to the tenants' garden.

Now where was that mouse the cat was stalking earlier? Was he over here under these plants that could be quickly dug up and tossed aside?

No.

Was he over here, on these squashed plants that a moment before the heavy dog had been standing upon?

Nope.

If you were to dig a hole approximately three feet deep with a two-foot diameter, would that reveal the miserable rodent?

No, indeed.

Maury next decided to investigate the garbage duct that the cat had run into earlier. *Mmm. Kind of flimsy material. Comes right off when you brush your shoulder against it.*

How about this part over here? Yeah, it dented up pretty good if you drummed your paws against it.

Well, better spray this useless piece of duct lying on the ground here. Leave it like this as a warning to the neighborhood dogs. Don't mess with Maury.

Don't even try.

Now to go over and pull the cat's legs off . . .

All of a sudden, in the distance, Maury heard a voice calling him. Hey, that was his temporary mistress's voice. *The heck with the cat,* Maury informed all and sundry. He had work to do.

Unfortunately, he was temporarily distracted from said work by his discovery of the Dumpster, which he found by following the path beyond the now-destroyed garbage chute.

What fun!

Once in this bin of doggy enjoyment, Maury set to work, ripping open the heavy green and black bags of garbage, burrowing deeply inside.

Hmmm. Undercooked spinach soufflé. Not bad at all. Especially mixed with this guy's overcooked hamburgers. Boy. You could do a lot worse than come to this Dumpster when it was time to dine.

Unfortunately now he was *really* thirsty. Well, no matter. There had to be a toilet around here somewhere.

Maury sniffed the air and smelled a baby and a box of laundry soap in the area.

Yum. Maury loved babies!

Padding into the little tenant washer and dryer room, Maury discovered an adorable little one-year-old named Eduardo, whom some mother had left alone for a moment while she ran upstairs to retrieve her forgotten roll of quarters.

Hello, baby! Maury greeted him.

The child looked into Maury's big face and answered quite happily in mental language, *Hello, Mr. Dog!*

Maury then pulled the water feed line out of the washing machine, wet his whistle, turned back to the young human biscuit and licked him avidly.

"Whee!" the little baby gurgled.

Having satisfied the child's need for affection temporarily, Maury stood up on the dryer. Finding the laundry soap box, Maury stuck his tongue in tentatively. Upon finding out that his hunch had been exactly right, and indeed he did not like the taste of the soap, he swatted the offending box across the room.

Look, Mr. Dog! Eduardo laughed delightedly. *Bubbles!*

And it was true. The rushing water from the washing machine was hitting the box of concentrated soap powder and was causing quite a little bubble bath.

Maury took a running start and slid across the room on the slippery floor, smashing into the folding table.

Baby Eduardo laughed. This was almost more fun than his tiny little body could hold.

All of a sudden a grinding noise was heard. Maury padded over to the ancient elevator and investigated. Someone was in this thing coming down.

"Mommy! Mommy!" Eduardo said excitedly. How delighted his mother would be when she saw how the doggy had made everything into a baby-fun wonderland!

Maury nodded. While technically the elevator box could hold any of the seventy-odd tenants of the building, it probably was Eduardo's mother. It had been Maury's experience in his short life that whenever you were really starting to have fun, mothers usually showed up to ruin things.

• • •

Mrs. Felix Cruz, "Mercedes" to her friends, wife of one of Palmer's premier homicide detectives, and mother to the gurgling baby downstairs in the laundry room, found herself trapped between the first and basement floors. This had happened as a consequence of Maury, that lovable, playful dog, opening up the gate to the elevator in the laundry room to see what he could smell.

Frantic with worry and beating herself up mentally for having abandoned her little Eduardo, even just to run upstairs for a moment, Mercedes picked up the elevator phone. She wished she could call her husband at the police station and have him come down and arrest the building management for not replacing those ancient prewar elevators. However, the phone could not dial out and was only connected to the super's apartment. Unfortunately, no one was picking up.

Mercedes slammed down the phone and then kicked the sidewalls of the elevator, invoking the names of several saints.

Who knew how long it would be before she was rescued? And what would happen to her baby?

Weeping in impotent fury, Mercedes pulled the alarm button.

Jackie returned to the apartment, breathless from running up the stairs. "Maury's not in the courtyard," she announced. "Where could he have gone?"

All of a sudden they heard the alarm ringing.

"That's not another fire alarm," Jackie worried at once.

"No, it's the elevator," Frances sighed. "Someone's stuck again. I guess the super isn't home tonight."

The alarm went on and on.

"Can't we do something?"

Frances groaned. She and her husband had assiduously avoided teaching their daughter any sense of social responsibility. They had never given to charities or watched telethons or tolerated, even for a moment, the phony rants of evangelists who were clearly more concerned with feathering their own nest than contributing to the needs of their brethren from distant lands. None of this had worked. Probably in rebellion to her sweet but rather self-centered parents, Jackie had become a do-gooder, a burden Frances often found uncomfortable to bear.

"All right," she allowed. "Let me get me keys."

At the same time, down in the laundry room, Maury, licking little Eduardo's feet and making the urchin laugh lustily with the sort of joy that tickling only brings to very small children, decided that he too should be on his way. But first, perhaps, he'd take a moment to gnaw on the flimsy canvas strap that held Eduardo in his little yellow seat contraption . . .

Suddenly Eduardo tumbled out of the seat, landing on the huge dog's back and grabbing on for dear life with his tiny hands.

Maury sighed. *All right. Just a quick one.*

Inside the elevator, Mercedes Cruz tried the telephone again.

Bingo Allen, having showered and yielded the bathroom to Donna Lee, heard his lover's phone ringing and cried out, "Donna! The phone!"

"What, dear?" she called back.

Bingo, like every man in history, ignored the fact that his lady love simply could not hear him when the shower was running, and repeated crabbily, "I said, 'The phone is ringing!' "

Donna Lee sighed and turned off the water, wrapped two towels around her and stuck her head out of the open bathroom door. "What is it, honey?"

"Damn it, Donna! Can't you hear? It's the phone!"

"Are you expecting a call?" Donna Lee asked considerately.

Most people would have hung up after around seven rings or so, but Mercedes, in the elevator downstairs, grimly held onto the receiver and let it go on. It gave her the illusion she was accomplishing something.

"No, I'm not expecting a call!" Bingo responded indignantly. "I wouldn't give out this number to anyone!"

Donna Lee grabbed the phone and immediately recognized the voice of her neighbor Mercedes.

"Help!" Mercedes said. "I'm stuck in the elevator!"

All of a sudden, from somewhere up above Mercedes, Frances Costello shouted down, "Hello in the elevator. We're here to help you!"

Mercedes tucked the phone to her ample chest. "Just a minute."

Donna Lee, a little annoyed to be put on hold by a woman trapped in the elevator, looked over to Bingo Allen, and noted for the first time that his fingernails were filthy. More filthy, clearly, than they could have become in the interval *since* the newspaperman and she had made love.

"What is it, sweetie?" Bingo asked obliviously.

"Just," Donna Lee's voice shook with rage, "go!"

"Mercedes!" Frances shouted. "It's Frances Costello, dear. Don't you worry. I'm up here with me daughter Jacqueline Shannon, and our friends, Bara and Jean and Marj. And a friend of Jackie's from Puerto Rico, Nancy Gordon!"

"Cosmo's wife?" Mercedes asked.

"We're divorced!" Nancy yelled down. "And I'm the big winner in the poker game so far."

"Woof."

"Oh—and Jake's here too!"

"Maybe if I just push the summons button," Jackie muttered.

"Don't be daft, daughter," Frances said at once. "You don't think she's pushed every button she can find in there?"

"She may have, Mother," Jackie agreed. "But the elevator panel doesn't open when one of the floor doors isn't completely shut. Maybe someone has noticed the open door by now, wherever it is, and shut it."

As if obeying his temporary mistress's words, Maury, on the floor below them, shoved the elevator door in the laundry room shut with his nose. That was all he needed, for the baby now riding uncomfortably on his back to fall down the shaft. There'd be heck to pay for that, boy.

"Whee!" Maury's small rider cried out, simultaneously expressing his joy at what he was experiencing and describing the substance that he was unleashing down the big dog's back.

Great! Maury thought to himself. How was he going to explain this to Jake?

CHAPTER 14

Bingo Allen, who had crossed paths with Jackie on his way out of the building, sat in the backseat with Jake, who dined on some slender beef strips from the party.

Maury, as usual, sat in the front seat, his vent window wide open, smelling about the way you'd expect a wet dog to smell, and listening to Lorne Greene sing "Johnny Ringo" on his cowboy tape.

"I still don't see what the big deal is," Bingo grumped.

"Oh, just call me an old stick in the mud," Jackie shot back over her right shoulder. "But I think sleeping with another man's wife in his own bed when he's out for the evening is pretty low."

"Yeah, like you're little Miss Perfect," Bingo sneered.

"I'm not going to waste my time defending myself, Bingo," Jackie said. "I'm just going to point out that Randy 'Macho Man' Botz has hair on his knuckles and a rap sheet as long as your . . . forearm."

Jake ducked his head under his car blanket and fell asleep.

"All right, all right," Bingo winced. "What will it take to buy your silence?"

"The upshot of it is," Bingo informed Jackie fifteen minutes later, "one of the animals in the zoo was killing people."

"What? Like Beau?"

Bingo shook his head. "I don't know. I got a tip."

"From Grover Gilmore?" Jackie asked quickly.

Bingo started to answer, then caught himself. "I really can't say."

"But doesn't that sound strange to you, Bingo?" Jackie asked. "Who do we know who died over at the zoo in the last few months?"

"Besides Grover?"

"Yes," Jackie said, sighing with relief as Maury's cowboy tape finally ended. "Besides Grover."

"I don't know," Bingo replied, "but then it's been a busy day. I'll have to get Matt Hannover at the paper to do a computer search for me."

"I'll ask around too," Jackie decided.

Bingo smiled. "I thought you weren't going to get involved?"

Jackie returned the smile. "Just till I go to Florida. Then I turn it over to the real detectives."

"Woof," Jake said sleepily.

Bingo laughed. "Your dogs?"

Jackie laughed with him. "Whoever can do the best job."

CHAPTER 15

The next morning came much too early. Maury, jealous that Jake could sleep inside the house and he couldn't, had barked half the night. When Jackie's neighbor Merida, infuriated by the noise, had finally opened her window and dumped a big pot of water on Maury, it had so delighted the big dog that he had then barked another two hours for another dousing.

As Jackie blearily looked at the first of the term papers she had to grade this morning, her computer's electronic mail icon started flashing.

Oh-oh, Jackie thought to herself. What had she done now?

Taking her mouse, which Peter, as a surprisingly thoughtful birthday present for his mom, had painted with Jackie's favorite, a figure of the black and white Mickey Mouse, she double-clicked for her message.

"Ms. Walsg," it said, indicating to Jackie that the person who was sending her this message had let their touch-typing skills atrophy a bit. "Please see

125

Mr. Bagh . . ." The message then went right off the screen.

"Oh, well," Jackie said to Mae West, whose photo poster hung on her wall. "I guess the chairman wants to see me."

Noticing the blinking light on her answering machine, she checked her messages there as well, and found that both her mother and her colleague Fred Jackson had been trying to get in touch with her. Fred wanted to beg her to look up Ivor Quest on her trip to Florida, where the communications department chairman was taking an extended personal leave, and convince him to return to Palmer. Frances, Jackie suspected, had just felt like nagging her a little.

Next, Jackie noticed a sheet of paper lying on the tray of her newly installed personal fax machine. It was a copy of the TV listings from today's paper, sent over by Thalia Gilmore to notify Jackie that she'd be appearing on that afternoon's special live edition of the *The Jerry Waring Show*.

Just as Jackie was beginning to muse on the old days when people wrote letters, the phone rang. It was her friend and neighbor, Merida Green.

"Did you hear about Thea Granville?" Merida asked. "She's in the hospital and she's really sick."

"Little Thea?" Jackie was simply astounded. She knew the young girl as a classmate of Peter's and his pal Isaac Cook at the Downtown Arts School. "What happened?"

"I don't know," Merida responded. "Some kind

of weird bug. Like that rat pee disease that's killing people in the Southwest.''

"She has that hantavirus?" Jackie wondered, shivering slightly. All her life Jackie had had a morbid fear of rodents. Now, if it turned out that these killer rats—Jackie couldn't help but wonder in passing if they had come from Central America too, like killer bees—were in Palmer, she fully intended to go to Florida on Sunday and never ever come back.

"No, something else. Not quite as bad—but they don't know what it is and if they can't identify it, then they don't know what medications to give her and she may die."

CHAPTER 16

"Jackie Walsh to see Mr. Baghorn."

The secretary buzzed the office. "Ms. Walsh is here, Marcus."

"Show her in, princess."

"Yes, darling." The secretary and the acting chairman had recently been married.

A little embarrassed by the display, Jackie stalked into the office.

Marcus Baghorn, a nattily dressed, Yiddish-speaking leprechaun of a man, popped to his feet to greet her.

"So, Jackie. Let me ask you straight out. Do you intend to apply your usual skills to the Palmer Zoo, you should excuse the expression, 'murder'?"

"I hadn't planned to put all of my efforts into it," Jackie said. "But I might be able to find out something that would help the police solve the killing of Grover Gilmore . . ."

"You know Morton Slake is in the hospital," Marcus commented, selecting a mint from his candy dish. "At death's door and trying various skeleton keys. A very sick boy our former City Council chairman is. Corky Dole, the district attorney, thinks he may have been poisoned.''

"Hmm,'' Jackie said. "Mort Slake's the head of the Wildlife Habitat Park these days, isn't he?''

Marcus Baghorn sat back in his chair. "He is if he pulls through. He was until yesterday.''

"Odd, isn't it?''

"What's that?'' Marcus asked. "That Morton Slake and Grover Gilmore both worked for the zoo?''

"What do you mean by that?'' Jackie asked at once.

"What did I say?'' Marcus wondered. "I was thinking that they both work at the zoo. It's a coincidence. What's the big deal?''

"I don't know that it is a big deal . . .'' Jackie started. "But when two people in a small town die who work in the same place, it seems suspicious. That's all. Particularly when a group of rich Palmerites want to see the Wildlife Park closed or moved. The escape of Beau is a good excuse.''

All of a sudden, their conversation was interrupted by a cry. They turned and saw Julia Granville, dark-haired film student, standing at the office door.

"Ms. Granville,'' Marcus said, surprised.

"Julia!'' Jackie exclaimed. "What's wrong?''

"I'm sorry to interrupt you . . . Mr. Baghorn . . . Ms. Walsh.'' Julia Granville wiped a tear from the corner of her eye. "And I didn't mean to startle you. It's just that I came in here to ask you if I could skip

classes for the rest of the week to be with my sister
. . . and I heard . . . I heard you talking about the
zoo."

Julia started to cry again.

"The zoo," Julia choked out, "was the last place
little Thea went before she got sick."

CHAPTER 17

After assuring Marcus that she wouldn't neglect her teaching duties in the pursuit of Palmer's latest wanted villain—and dropping poor Julia off at the hospital—Jackie stopped off at the Juniper Tavern.

Corky Dole, holding a beer mug, cleared his throat to gain the film instructor's attention.

"District Attorney Dole," Jackie said brightly. "Touch of bronchitis?"

"I hope not," he answered tiredly. "I'm pumped full of antibiotics just so I don't get whatever felled poor Mort Slake. Mind if I sit down?"

Jackie nodded curtly, but didn't bother removing her shoulder bag from his seat. Jackie wasn't trying to be rude exactly, but on the other hand she did not particularly want to talk. Especially when she was eating. Perhaps if DA Dole was uncomfortable sitting across from her he would come more rapidly to the point.

"What's on your mind, Mr. Dole?" Jackie snapped. "Talk quickly. I've got an appointment."

"All right," Corky said, fumbling desperately to

keep Jackie's bag from falling to the ground. "I don't suppose you're sniffing around on this Palmer Wildlife Habitat Park matter?"

"My dog sniffs around, Mr. Dole," Jackie said. "When I help the police solve a crime, I do it with intelligence, persistence, and the experience of someone who's lived in this town for most of her life."

"Yeah, well, that's the point, Ms. Walsh," Corky said, leaning forward. "You know how it is down at the DA's. We can't use the talents you wonderful amateurs use. Supreme Court and all that. Generally my people just try to build a case against the first person the police bring in, even if it turns out later that the suspect just happened to be walking by the crime site on his way to buy a paper."

"It's his own damn fault," Jackie interrupted. "He should have gotten a home subscription."

"Exactly!" Corky replied.

"So what's your point?" Jackie asked.

"People are buzzing that Morton Slake is the one who let Beau loose to kill Grover Gilmore."

Jackie raised one eyebrow, a trick she had learned just to unnerve men. "Why would he do that?"

"He and Grover Gilmore were always arguing about the treatment of the animals," Corky shrugged. "There were some deaths that might have been preventable. Including a little newborn hippo."

"That's terrible," Jackie said, quickly swallowing a mouthful of potato and sour cream.

"Yeah." Corky took a mighty swig. He was determined to get drunk.

"And everyone's hearing about the Palmer Group being interested in tearing down the zoo and moving the animals into the theme park."

"Why would anyone think Morton Slake was in favor of that?" Jackie wondered.

"He's in city government. They just naturally assume that he's pond slime," Corky pointed out.

"And if he dies of his disease? What *is* wrong with him anyway?" Jackie asked.

"They don't know," Corky shrugged. "It's a strange virus. It came upon him so suddenly I thought he'd been poisoned. Apparently a few people have come down with the same thing. Kids, mostly."

"A little girl named Granville by any chance?"

"Maybe so," Corky said. "That sounds familiar, but I don't know all of them. They're in bad shape though. They're doing all they can to help them, but it's rough."

"It's not that I'm not interested, Corky," Jackie said, softening. "I just don't know what I could do. It sounds, doesn't it, that if anyone stood to gain by all this, it would be the Palmer Group. You don't really want to go after them, do you?"

"Your point? Of course I wouldn't be happy to have to try to indict a bunch of city fathers, but let's get this thing solved and let the chips fall where they may."

"All right," Jackie answered, happy to see that the DA had some shred of human dignity left in him.

"I don't know how they could have managed to get Morton Slake sick, but . . ."

Jackie scooped up the last of her steak sauce with a bit of toast, then resumed. "If we assume that the two are related, then we have to factor in the children. I talked to Julia Granville today and she said her sister Thea visited the zoo just before she got sick. Perhaps there's a common thread there. Perhaps there is some animal there who got people sick, including Morton Slake."

Corky sat back heavily in his seat. Despite his efforts, he had never felt more sober in his life. "You mean they wanted Morton Slake dead, not Grover Gilmore?"

Jackie shrugged. "It's a place to start. As with the killing of Sadie, it's a hard crime to pin on someone. Wait. . . . maybe that's it."

"What?" Corky asked.

As if on cue, Jake trotted over.

Jackie got to her feet and craned her neck for the waitress.

"It looks like you've got an idea on how to solve this case, but you're not telling me what it is," Corky Dole said, somewhat befuddled.

"Gotta run," Jackie said, taking the check from the waitress and heading for the register.

"Wait." Corky lurched after Jackie as she and Jake made for the door.

They emerged onto the bright white sidewalk. "You can't," he bleated hotly, "just leave me like this."

Jackie half turned. "Corky, you're five minutes

from your office. If you're not up to walking, take a cab."

"No, I mean . . . we need help. The police are running all over town like a bunch of Keystone Kops, answering calls from people who think they heard or saw the giant killer ostrich . . . Please, Jackie," the pathetic DA continued to beg. "I haven't got the slightest clue how to proceed with this investigation. It's like you said before, my best suspect for killing Grover is in the hospital. My best suspects for doing something to make Mort Slake sick are the most powerful untouchables in town.

"The worst of it is," Corky continued, finally managing to locate his sunglasses and put them on, "that my best special investigator is out in Hollywood working as a technical adviser on that *CopLady* comeback film with Celestine Barger."

Jackie at least had the good grace to feel bad about that part. It had been, as Dole indicated, Jackie's long-time writing partner Celestine's idea to co-opt Michael McGowan, the Homicide captain who had once solved crimes with Jackie (for a short time, the two had been romantically involved, but that had withered on the vine). However, the script, *CopLady! Back with a Vengeance*, was a full collaboration between the two writers, the first script they had managed to sell to Hollywood after a dry spell that despite their early success in the business had kept the team in Palmer, teaching and raising their families, for years.

"I'm sorry, Corky, that he's been kept away from his job for so long. You wouldn't believe the problems and delays they've had doing that picture.''

Dole brushed away Jackie's sympathy. "I know, I know. I'm begging for help here, Jackie.''

"All right, Corky," Jackie said, opening the door of her Jeep to let Jake into the back. "Here's what I think you should do. Seal up the zoo. Post policemen until we can bring in someone to carefully go over the grounds and find out if whatever was making people sick is still there. And if you find anyone who might have seen something, you can send them to me if you like. I'll give you the number of my cellular phone. I'll be glad to help out in any way I can. You know, one of these days you're going to have to put me on the payroll.''

"Bless you," Corky said sincerely.

Jackie gave the DA a look, then continued, "Have Lee Humphries, the medical examiner, do tests on Grover Gilmore. See if he had whatever Morton Slake has. You might get any zoo employee who came into contact with Morton Slake tested too.

"Find Sadie's body. Get a vet to perform an autopsy on Sadie and see if she had some bug that might have infected the others.''

Corky fumbled for a pad and started writing Jackie's instructions down. As he came to the last one, he raised his head to ask, "What makes you think Sadie was the infected animal?''

"Hoss Greenaway told me that she was sick," Jackie recalled. "He said that was why they separated Beau away from her. And it gives someone a reason to kill her. After all, if the animal had been buried without being examined, it would have certainly disposed of the evidence. What else?''

Jackie looked at Jake.

The big dog stuck out a paw, tapping Jackie's car keys. "Oh, sure. And find out who had access to the keys and used them to open the cages in the Aviary-Simian House. How hard would it be for someone to lift a key, or make a copy, or to pick the lock without one?''

"Thanks, Jackie. It never hurts to get an extra brain on the case. There's a lot of pressure to get this solved. I guess people don't like to think of the zoo as a place where bad things can happen."

"Glad to help."

"And somehow it seems like you always know how to ask the right questions."

"Bring on the suspects," said Jackie. "And if my grilling doesn't work, we can always ask that TV spy Ronald Dunn to give 'em the old rubber hose."

"Great, I'd love to meet him. Ron Dunn, I mean."

"Yeah," Jackie remarked, preparing to take her hasty leave, "I'd like to spend a little more time with him myself."

CHAPTER 18

Jake, because of his near-celebrity status, had been allowed to sit by his mistress in the back corner of the studio where *The Jerry Waring Show* took place. Obviously hot under the powerful overhead lights, Jake lay quietly, conserving his energy.

Finally, after an interminable wait, the host made his appearance.

"People!" he yelled.

"People care!" the audience roared back. They would have said anything, just to be on TV.

"And today, ladies . . ." Jerry Waring peered out into the audience like an Indian scout looking for buffalo. "It is just ladies, isn't it? No fellows in the audience again today?"

"Put on somebody they want to watch and they'll turn out," a male voice called out.

"Ha, ha, okay . . ." Jerry Waring pretended to agree when he saw that the speaker was a three-hundred-pound stage grip. Jerry Waring knew that the crew hated his guts, but he was endlessly willing to put up with their taunts for fear of having a lighting instrument come down on his head.

"Anyway, ladies, we got one heckuva show for you today."

The audience applauded until their hands hurt.

"First up, we've got an update on the happenings down at the Palmer Wildlife Habitat Park. We also have on the program today Rayburn Herman."

Upon hearing his name, the plump, pleasant-looking man raised an arm to wave to the camera and elbowed, slightly, the woman sitting next to him.

"And Jane Bellamy, the mayor of Palmer."

The camera swung to the mayor, looking unnaturally tan and wearing a bright red wig. Normally, the mayor was fairly self-composed. Today however Jane Bellamy could barely manage a professional smile.

"And," the host's voice took on a dramatic tone, "animal activist Ms. Thalia Gilmore."

There was a break while a couple of commercials were aired. Bored, Jackie fidgeted and absentmindedly petted Jake.

"We're back," Jerry Waring announced, "with Jane Bellamy, the present mayor of Palmer, and . . ."

The mayor smiled a sickly grin and tried not to react to the jab.

"Rayburn Herman of the Animal Rights Lobby."

The big man mopped his face with a paper tissue and smiled.

"And Thalia Gilmore, mother of the victim and

committed animal-rights supporter.''

Thalia dabbed at her eyes.

"But first let's go to the scene at the Aviary-Simian House.''

The camera showed a field reporter in front of Gooey's cage in the zoo. "I'm here, Jerry. And I'm standing in front of Gooey the baby gorilla's cage. It was right here on this spot that Morton Slake collapsed to the ground . . .''

Gooey the gorilla was reaching through the bars now, trying to shake hands, but succeeding only in knocking the microphone out of the reporter's grasp.

Recovering from the sudden clumsy silence, Waring approached the stage. "And now, folks, let's talk to the victim's mother for a moment, shall we? Thalia Gilmore. How are you?''

"It's still a terrible shock,'' Thalia responded. "But everyone's been very good to me.''

"Ever see this before?'' Jerry Waring said at once, waving a sawed-off golf club in front of Thalia Gilmore's face.

The older woman was startled by the odd threatening act, and the audience gasped.

"Well, I suppose I saw it on that news program last night.''

"You saw it being used to bludgeon Sadie the ostrich to death, Ms. Gilmore?''

"Er . . . yes?'' Thalia knew that the scene depicted on the television had been a reenactment, carefully scripted and performed by professionals, but she didn't know whether she should mention that.

"Well, I should tell you straight out,'' Jerry Waring said, speaking quickly, "that there is no reason to believe that this is the weapon. It is, after all, a prop that was used for the news broadcast reenactment, so it was not necessarily the weapon that was used on poor Sadie. But if it *was*, Mrs. Gilmore . . ." Thalia nodded to show that she was following along, though she really wasn't.

"Then who . . . ?" Jerry Waring let his mighty chest fill with air. "Who would logically have such a weapon?"

"Well." Thalia was a little taken aback by the question, but she blurted out, "A golfer?"

"A golfer!" Jerry Waring exclaimed. "Yes, I agree, Mrs. Gilmore. And who should know better than the victim's dear widowed mother?"

The police, Jackie thought to herself.

"Mayor Jane Bellamy." Jerry Waring stuck his microphone in front of her face. "This weapon looks to be a golf club, wouldn't you say?"

Jane Bellamy, a little confused as to why she should be identifying a prop that had just been established not to be the murder weapon of Sadie anyway, paused for a moment. "Yes, it does," she admitted.

Jerry Waring smiled. "Do you recognize this woman, Madam Mayor?"

A picture of a woman in golfing clothes flashed on the studio monitor.

"That appears to be Elizabeth McKean Curtis," Jane answered tiredly.

"Right on the first try," Jerry Waring sneered. He seemed to be smiling, but no, there was no mistake about it. It was a sneer. "Ms. Curtis is a golfer, is she not?"

"I really have no idea," Jane Bellamy lied.

Jackie knew the answer to that—and the answer was a decided yes. In fact, Liz Curtis, now involved with Jackie's ex-husband Cooper, was renowned for her prowess on the links.

Jerry Waring turned to the audience. "Liz Curtis is a golfer." He then turned back to the mayor. "Ms. Curtis, her ex-husband, former mayor Bill Curtis, and her sister, Phyllis McKean Greenaway, are all on the board of McKean Beverages, aren't they?"

"I suppose they are, yes," Jane Bellamy answered dryly. "Really, Mr. Waring. I am not an expert on corporate boards."

"Well, surely, you're at least familiar with the boards you sit on, Mayor Bellamy?"

"I am on the board of McKean. Yes. It is primarily an honorary position, attained from a lifetime of work in the academic sector—before I entered politics. I have not attended many meetings and as long as the city does business with McKean Beverages, who supply the soft drinks . . ."

"And soft drink machines," Jerry Waring pointed out.

"Yes, well." Jane Bellamy maintained a relative cool, but it was clear that she was making an effort to do so. "One doesn't usually find soft drinks lying on the floor, you know? One generally does have to go to a store or machine to purchase one."

"And you are also on the board of Seattle-Style Cappuccino, are you not?"

"Yes," Mayor Bellamy said forthrightly.

"And Seattle-Style Cappuccino is owned by the McKeans and Mr. Frank Dill. Is it not?"

"Yes."

"And you are also on the board of Dill Dog Chow, are you not?"

"Yes, I suppose I am, Mr. Waring," Jane Bellamy answered.

"And Mr. Dill is also on the corporate boards of McKean Beverages and Seattle-Style Cappuccino?"

"Yes, Mr. Waring—I take your point." Jane Bellamy popped a stick of gum into her mouth before resuming. "There are a half dozen of us or so who belong to a group called the Palmer Group. We are on interlocking corporate boards. There is nothing sinister about this. It is a quite common practice, in fact. You'll notice that the businessmen who serve on each other's boards are not in competition with each other. McKean Beverages, for instance, is in direct competition with Goodwillie Good Water. You'll notice that they are not on each other's boards. Obviously for those of us who are not in competition with each other, there is some benefit in having people who know something about business being on your corporate board. For instance, Frank Dill theoretically shares with Max Greenaway the way he handles his incinerator fume problem, and Sam Sharpe can discuss with Liz Curtis how he handles certain interstate trucking hauls, and so on. I fail to see . . ."

"And what would your connection be to these people, Mayor Bellamy?"

"Well, we are old friends, many of us," Jane Bellamy conceded reluctantly. "Some of these people I met through my husband Richard Bellamy . . . he is the head of Marx-Wheeler Medical Center, of course. Others I met through the Symphony Society where Phyllis Greenaway and Liz Curtis and myself . . ."

"I understand you are a charter member of the Palmer Group," Jerry Waring interrupted. "But what was your, er, *contribution* to the original group, do you think?"

"I resent that," Jane Bellamy said at once.

"You were added to the Palmer Group because of your background in urban planning. Is that not correct, Mayor Bellamy?"

Jackie, like many of the women in the audience, was a little confused about where all this was going, but she was impressed, whatever the relevance to the killing of poor Grover Gilmore, with how many different projects Jane Bellamy had involved herself in. There were very few women in the world who could parley a small investment into hundreds of thousands of dollars and it was awe-inspiring to see it happen right here in Jackie's own hometown.

"Yes, Mr. Waring," Jane Bellamy answered tiredly. "I was added to the Palmer Group because of some theoretical model planning I did for a doctoral thesis at Rodgers University."

"Your model—do you mind if we put a picture of it up here on the monitor for the audience to take a look at, Madam Mayor?"

Jane Bellamy looked into Jerry Waring's eyes and

said, "I suppose that would be all right."

The impressive model of the "Palmer of the Future" as envisioned by Jane Bellamy over a decade earlier was flashed on-screen, and the audience applauded. It was very professional-looking.

"As you can see, people," Jerry Waring said, "the model is very similar to the outlay of today's Palmer. Is that a coincidence, Mayor Bellamy, or has your influence on the movers and shakers of Palmer resulted in them consciously taking your design and implementing it?"

Jane Bellamy took a sip from her soda. "A combination of both, I would say."

"That would have been my guess too." Jerry Waring smiled. "You predicted that the Palmer Regular Steel Foundry would be closed, five years or so before it actually did go under?"

Jane nodded. "The financial literature during those days was full of dire predictions for the Rust Belt and its steel and manufacturing-related industries."

Waring nodded. "You predicted that the Foundry would be replaced by a shopping mall."

"Still possible, I suppose," Jane confirmed. "Loss of interstate funds to refurbish the West Palmer Thruway hurt the possibilities of that, of course."

"And here, in this very building, I notice there is a new Symphony Hall."

Jane Bellamy nodded again. "We are hoping that if Alton Turner can do for our symphony what he did for the one in Seattle that they will be the main tenants here, and we may be able to expand the parking facilities."

"And what would happen to *The Jerry Waring Show*, Madam Mayor," Waring asked, half-serious. "Under your plan, I mean?"

"I suppose you would have to find new studio space, Mr. Waring," Jane answered with complete equanimity.

"Preferably as far away from you as possible, eh, Mayor?" Waring teased heavy-handedly.

"Your words, not mine," Mayor Bellamy answered with a wintry smile. "Your blithe willingness to blame everything on businessmen is somewhat understandable, I suppose, since there are some businessmen who are less concerned with selling actual goods and services than with just manipulating money. Myself, I do not much like those kinds of businessmen or women, I should add, and do not associate with them. As much as you'd like to disbelieve me, Mr. Waring, I am not just another corrupt politician."

Mayor Bellamy waited for the muttered reactions that she, as a seasoned politician, knew would come, then resumed, "Have you ever wondered why people like Bill Curtis leave office far richer than when they went in? Seems hard to believe they could do such things, if they really did put their investments in blind trusts before they took office or if they were simply saving the amount they accrued from their modest politician's salaries.

"That was one of the reasons I ran for mayor. I ran because I had a vision for this town. A vision I

kept in this head for twenty years, and when I saw
that there was no one with a pure vision interested
in governing this town, then I put myself forward as
a reluctant last resort. I think that my story is rather
well known, Mr. Waring, and I am surprised that you
want to use so much of your precious airtime re-
hashing it, but I am not ashamed of a single act I've
committed since I've taken office.

"Ask your studio audience. I don't believe in
polls, because I know how easily they can be rigged,
but I do believe I am still relatively popular in this
town."

Jerry Waring looked to his audience, and they,
poor souls, not knowing what to do, and not wanting to incur the wrath of their host, did nothing.

"Well." Jane Bellamy's mouth drew into a thin
line. "I am still popular whether you permit your
audience to applaud or not."

Jerry Waring crossed his arms. "Oh. I think it's
perfectly permissible for these good people to
clap."

The overflow crowd burst into a firestorm of applause.

"Permissible," Waring continued with impecca-
ble timing, "but perhaps not really the best choice
under the circumstances."

The applause died so abruptly that Jackie looked
around to see if anyone was running up and down
the aisles lopping off hands.

"It's just that . . ." Jerry Waring said calmly and
dispassionately, "I notice, Mayor Bellamy, that on
your little model here, there is no Palmer Zoo."

CHAPTER 19

Jackie, still sitting in the studio waiting out another commercial break, reached down and quietly answered her buzzing cellular phone. "Hello?"

"Oh, the Good Lord preserve a poor dying woman . . ."

"Mother!" Jackie whispered. "I can't talk now. I'm at *The Jerry Waring Show.* I'll call you later."

"But wait a minute, dear," Frances bleated. "You didn't give me a chance to tell you what I've been calling and calling about."

"Sorry, Mom. Gotta run." Jackie clicked off and checked in on Jake. "I'm getting some ideas, boy. How about you?"

Jake nodded sagely.

Back from the break, Jerry Waring smiled toothily as the camera eye found him, then turned to Rayburn Herman. "Mr. Herman, your group has attracted a lot of attention over the years."

"Yes, Jerry," Herman responded heartily. "As we talk about in our recent book . . ."

"We're not talking about book plugs here, Rayburn," Jerry Waring snapped. "We're talking about murder. Two people are dead, Mr. Herman."

"Two?"

"Morton Slake died during the commercial break."

The audience fell silent for a moment in sober contemplation. It was an undistinguished end to a checkered career.

"Jeez . . . I'm sorry . . . I didn't know."

"Didn't know?" Waring nearly shouted at his guest. "Or didn't care?! Isn't it true, Mr. Herman, that your group protested experimentation on dogs at four targeted northeastern United States locations, successfully forcing the universities to move the site of their experimentation to Mexico where the whole project had to be started all over again? And of course there in Mexico, less effective laboratory procedures resulted in four times as many animals being sacrificed?

"How do you react to this, Mr. Herman?" Waring lashed out. "How can you in good conscience proceed when the results are calamitous to the very animals you allegedly wish to protect?"

Herman grew red-faced and the hitherto inoffensive-appearing man gave a hint of the way he must have looked back in the days of being a much-decorated marine sergeant and prisoner of war in Southeast Asia.

"I know that when we found out they had relocated the experimentation center, my people went down to Mexico and protested there as well. They protested and continued the protest even after the

Federales beat some of our people so badly that poor Luther Bonin cannot talk to this day.''

''We're wandering away from the point here, Mr. Herman,'' Jerry Waring barked. ''The fact of the matter is, your efforts, such as in that case, have caused more harm than good. Isn't that true?''

''It's not as true as you seem to imply, Mr. Waring,'' Herman said loudly. ''Most of the time when we intervene to save animals, we succeed. We may not succeed every time, and we seldom succeed in saving every animal, but we try, sir. Not every attempt to do good succeeds. Particularly when you are striving against a more powerful opposing force, but it is better to try and fail than never to try at all. Every time we have sued companies or even the federal government to stop abusing animals, our suits have had some impact. Even when we lost, we succeeded in shaming or scaring the offenders into abusing animals a little less. It's a start.''

''The dogs, Mr. Herman,'' Jerry Waring said firmly. ''What happened to the dogs in the American cardiac experiment? What happened to them?''

Herman swallowed his rage and then answered calmly. ''Well, a lot of the ones who had been experimented on were put to sleep. The healthier dogs were all put up for adoption. Many of them found good homes and have gone on to live long and happy lives.''

''And the ones who did not find adoptive homes, Mr. Herman?''

''I suppose they were put into the usual dog care system, Mr. Waring,'' Herman remarked tersely.

"Shelters and places of that sort."

"And if they were not claimed within a certain time, they were gassed as well?"

"That's the way we choose to handle unwanted animals in this civilization, Mr. Waring," Herman answered. "I don't approve of the system, but I think it's a lot more humane than subjecting them to painful and pointless experiments."

"Pointless?" Waring asked.

"The canine cardiorespiratory system bears no real relation to our own," Herman responded. "Scientists know this but they keep on experimenting regardless, because they have to do a certain amount of research and publishing to keep their academic appointments and because dogs are a lot less expensive than truly valuable laboratory animals like monkeys or chimpanzees."

"How valuable are baby gorillas, Mr. Herman?" Waring asked.

"In terms of money?" Herman considered for a moment. "I would say a healthy baby gorilla, and by healthy I mean a female baby gorilla whose reproductive system works normally, is worth thirty or forty thousand dollars. Since reproduction, not quality of life, is so important to us Americans, more than half the testing that goes on is simply to determine what effect a drug has on a pregnant mother and her baby. In terms of species survival, a healthy gorilla male is the more valuable animal. For some reason, most baby gorillas born in captivity are female, so a male, capable of reproducing itself four or five times in a lifetime, is worth its weight in gold."

Jerry Waring nodded skeptically, as if he were half-convinced that Herman was making up the entire thing, then asked, "The health of apes concerns you, Mr. Herman?"

"Yes, of course it concerns me, Mr. Waring," Herman growled, wiping the sweat from his face angrily, "which if you'd read any two pages of my book, you would know. The ape population is declining. When it gets too low, then the gene pool shrinks and you end up with cousins mating with cousins with the resulting genetic defects. This is serious business, not just for them, but for us. If we lose our closest kin in the animal kingdom, then we will not only lose a walking, living text on primitive man, but we lose an opportunity that may exist to communicate with these animals directly and perhaps through them with other animals, all the living animals in this world. I'm sure we can learn something from each and every one."

"You make your theoretical points very eloquently, Mr. Herman," Jerry Waring conceded. "But oftentimes in this complicated society noble aims fall short and end up becoming acts of wanton and malicious destruction." He then flipped to the next card. "Take the case of . . ."

"Please," Rayburn Herman said at once. "That list of yours. Who gave it to you? Some makeup manufacturing company, a pet store chain, a professional animal breeders' lobby? I've heard their charges. If you'll read our book, you'll see a lot of careful point by point refutations of these incidents that they keep trotting out to embarrass us. These people are professionals, Mr. Waring. They abuse or exploit animals for their own purpose and then put out a bunch of slick lies to explain away their actions, or to discredit groups that take issue with their actions. We make mistakes. We're amateurs. We screw up sometimes. People get hurt sometimes. But if you want a list of animals getting hurt, I can guarantee you I can supply a list a lot longer than that one and read you accounts of animal atrocities that would turn your stomach. And they'll never be able to make a credible claim that they were even *trying* to do the right thing.''

Waring looked into Rayburn Herman's eyes, nodded, and then dropped his cards into the side pocket of his suit jacket. ''All right, Mr. Herman. We'll give your group credit for sincerity, anyway. Why don't you tell the people at home what made you, Rayburn Herman, get into the animal rights movement?''

''Me?'' Herman shifted in his chair. Clearly the middle-aged man was uncomfortable talking about himself. ''Er, well . . .''

This put the largely female audience at ease. They were used to large, bald, heavyset men who had trouble expressing their feelings or revealing anything of substance about themselves.

''Did you always have pets growing up?'' Jerry Waring prompted.

''Uh, no. We wanted them. My mother and I, but my father . . . Well, he had a drinking problem and we never ended up having any."

Waring nodded. Of course he was profiling the man in his mind. After sixteen years of interviewing people of every conceivable physical and psychological type, Jerry Waring had learned a few techniques about how to handle certain people. Once he discovered which type they were, that is.

"Well, do you have pets now?" Jerry Waring asked, giving the animal rights activist enough rope to hang himself.

"No, I don't have any pets at the moment. No, not really. No."

Jerry Waring looked around as if bewildered by the answer. "I'm not sure I understand you, Mr. Herman? You advocate compassionate treatment of animals. Why should our viewers dig deep in their overtaxed pockets for the wherewithal to support other people's unwanted pets when the people leading these pro-animal movements aren't willing to do the same? Doesn't this smack of the hypocrisy, Mr. Herman, your poor misunderstood critics often accuse you of?"

"No, sir," Rayburn Herman answered at once. "It does not. My situation is unique. Obviously most of the members of our group have a great many pets whom they love dearly. I am a single man. I travel most of the time. I live in a small apartment. I don't have the room or the time to properly take care of an animal in my own residence. As someone who has seen what it does to an animal to keep it in too tight a space, to not give it the nourishment and the attention an animal needs, I am determined not to make the same mistakes. When I'm at home for any length of time, I put in long hours at one of our Animal Care Farms, feeding and caring for animals. Training them . . ."

"Training them, Mr. Herman?" Jerry Waring again feigned astonishment. "Shouldn't these poor animals be left to cavort and run free?"

"Of course not," Rayburn Herman snapped. "We try to give animals who might otherwise be cooped up in some apartment or laboratory or city pound an opportunity to run around a little and stretch their legs. At the same time we also give animals, dogs especially, a chance to work. Obviously a working pet is easier to place in some situations than a passive pet."

"He's right, Jake," Jackie said, bending over to her dog. "A crime-solving canine like you would be a much easier dog to place than a big goofy dog who can't do anything."

Jackie didn't rate a hand lick for that one. Talk about a left-pawed compliment.

"All right," Jerry Waring conceded. "I'm sure your group does do good work. Obviously no one would have put up with the kind of nonsense you pulled when you didn't use good judgment if you weren't also doing something right. What I'm asking is what about you? Why are you specifically interested in animals? What makes Rayburn Herman a man who dedicated himself to the welfare of animals instead of some equally worthy cause?"

Herman considered for a long moment. The audience couldn't quite tell whether he was deciding whether or not he was going to answer, or whether it was simply a matter of putting a complicated answer into words. Finally, one of the lightbulbs on one of the overhead lamps blew with a dull thud, and people jumped, then laughed, as the tension was broken.

"Well, I suppose it stems from the time I was a P.O.W. in Viet Nam," Herman said finally. "Our cages, cells, whatever you want to call them, weren't any too big. When I came back to the States it sickened me to see anything cooped up and miserable, like most animals are cooped up."

"And that's what made you join the cause?" Jerry Waring pressed.

"It's a little more complicated than that," Herman responded. "But that's the upshot, yes. I joined an animal liberation group because I hated to see things penned up."

"And you broke animals out of labs, and factories, and in some cases out of private animal owners' houses and businesses?"

"We're not thieves, Mr. Waring," Herman protested. "The few times we tried to free an animal from a bad situation in a private home or business, we didn't disappear with the animal. We simply used that tool as a lever to bring the animal abuse to the attention of the police. Oftentimes, they saw the conditions that led to our action and the bad owner was forced to clean up his act. And most of our actions were against academic or business institutions mistreating animals."

"Not zoos?"

"No." Herman's sincerity could be plainly seen on his face. "I think we learned from our mistakes or the mistakes of others in the past. There's not much point to freeing zoo animals. They can't survive outside of their controlled environments very long. What would be the point of freeing a koala when the only thing in the world he can survive on is eucalyptus trees and no eucalyptus grows in the United States?"

"What about ostriches, Mr. Herman?" Jerry Waring asked bluntly.

"We didn't set Beau free, Mr. Waring," Herman replied, equally blunt. "And we didn't kill his mate Sadie, either."

Jerry Waring turned to the audience. "Do you have any questions for Mr. Herman?"

A woman in the second row stood up. "Yes, Mr. Herman. Your group aren't those people that wanted to put drawers on the donkeys and such?"

"No, ma'am," Herman answered patiently. "That was Mr. Arbus's group. They are professional jokesters."

"I have a question for Mr. Herman," said a woman in the back.

Waring shielded his eyes and saw Jackie waving her arm. "Yes?"

Jackie smiled and asked, "I'd like to ask Mr. Herman why he came to Palmer and how long he has been here."

"I came here, ma'am, to plug my book," Herman answered easily. "Ms. Jacobs on the . . . well, I guess the other station."

"Station KCIN," Jerry Waring supplied willingly. "It's all right, Mr. Herman. They're a perfectly good station. Heck, they're the second or third best station in town."

Waring's audience laughed obligingly. They'd heard the joke plenty of times before.

"Anyway," Herman concluded. "I was supposed to be interviewed by her and then she got hurt, you know?"

A couple of the audience looked blank but then Jerry Waring reminded them, "Marcella Jacobs was the woman who was with Grover Gilmore when he got hurt. She was working undercover at the time."

A housewife with limp hair and a fondness for Peter Pan collars stood up. "I have a question for Mr. Herman."

"Ah, Ms. Blue, isn't it?"

Alice Blue was always looking for a cause to devote herself to. She had decided, finally, that if Jackie Walsh could solve crimes and get nice write-ups in the papers, so could she. So far she hadn't been very successful.

This time, however, Alice, who had taken more pains to go down to the zoo and to talk to many of the principals of the case, had a much better chance of solving it. Her question in fact was, "What did Ms. Jacobs go undercover to investigate?"

Jerry Waring turned to Rayburn Herman.

"I have no idea," was his reply.

"She didn't mention to you that she was investigating troubles down at the zoo and that's why she couldn't meet with you?" Alice pressed. "Seems like

that would have given her a perfectly good excuse
for putting you off a day or so."

"I guess most TV people don't figure they have
to come up with a good explanation for canceling
out on an author," Herman replied. "They figure
they're doing us a favor, and if we don't like it, too
bad."

While Alice Blue gave way to another woman who
wanted to know which makeup companies were still
doing allergy testing with laboratory animals, Jackie
quietly rose from her seat and stole out of the auditorium with her faithful dog.

Alice Blue had been on the right track, Jackie
thought to herself. She should have asked Marcella
herself when they were together yesterday at Marx-
Wheeler, but she had just assumed that Grover Gilmore had been killed before telling Marcella
whatever it was that was going wrong at the Palmer
Wildlife Habitat Park.

Now that she thought about it, Jackie realized that
Alice Blue was right. Clearly Marcella wouldn't have
gone to the trouble of going undercover and de-
voting at least an afternoon of her time to the story
unless she had at least been given a hint as to what
was there. Presumably there was some question of
the animals being abused, but there would have had
to be more than that to attract Marcella Jacobs to
investigate at such length. Either there was a pattern
of systematic abuse and Marcella was trying to tie it
into the higher-ups such as Morton Slake, or perhaps there had been animals abused and zoo officials like Slake had been actively involved in

covering up the crimes and disposing of the evidence for fear that this would be used as an excuse by the Palmer Group to close the zoo and open a theme park on the spot.

So the question was not what Marcella was doing at the Palmer Wildlife Habitat Park. Jackie believed Rayburn Herman when he pointed out that there wasn't any real reason for Marcella to confide in him. The better question was—assuming Marcella knew enough to go on the air and level a few accusations—what was she waiting for now?

Was the KCIN newswoman simply waiting for the suspense to build, before going back to work? Marcella had confided to Jackie that this was her first real vacation in almost five years and that for once, she wasn't going to try to set any records getting out of her comfortable hospital bed and going back to work.

But still, someone was already dead, thanks to Beau. Sadie had been brutally murdered by someone, and perhaps the sicknesses of Morton Slake and Thea Granville were related to what was happening down at the zoo. Someone needed to do something, Jackie thought, or there was a distinct possibility that someone else would get hurt. Jackie got into her Jeep. Jake, now alert and rested, sniffed the air and started attuning himself to clue hunting.

Jackie looked at her watch. She had exactly one hour to investigate before she had to be at the Radio Arts Building to watch Ron Dunn's dress rehearsal. It probably wasn't enough time to solve the crime, but . . .

It was enough time to try.

CHAPTER 20

The first stop was the *Chronicle*. Fortunately for Jackie, Matt Hannover, a very attractive man who could have gotten work on a soap opera if he bothered to get his teeth fixed, was working late in the computer room.

Jackie noted, as she came in, the computer expert's thick wool pants, green pullover rugby shirt top, and the light blue Goretex vest he was wearing, and figured that this was some sort of "Hi, I'm a computer nerd five days a week, but on weekends I play hockey" look.

Then, after a few moments of standing in the computer room, which had been cooled to fifty-five degrees in order to make the big mainframes work more efficiently, she regretted her elegant but flimsy black Versace outfit and wished that she too had dressed for ice fishing.

"You must be Matt," Jackie said.

"I could have been anyone," the intense young giant said, not bothering to get up from his chair. "Who are you?"

"Jackie Walsh, I'm . . ."

Matt Hannover stopped listening and called up a file on his computer. In a moment Jackie's face and vital statistics appeared in front of him.

"Here we go, you're 'Palmer's Amateur Sleuth Extraordinaire.' "

"Yeah, well." Jackie smiled her crooked smile. "I'd like to think of myself as a woman on her way to Florida, but that remains to be seen. Is it possible to maybe turn up the heat for a moment?"

Hannover gave her the sort of look that Spock used to give mere mortals and answered, "No. Now what's on your mind, Ms. Walsh?"

"You can call me Jackie."

"I could call you Fred. I take it you're looking for Bingo Allen?"

"Actually . . ."

Hannover pressed a couple of buttons. "Charles Allen checked out at 4:37. He was going to meet SC#2."

"What's 'SC' mean?" Jackie asked quickly.

"Secret Contact," Hannover said with some disdain. "A source."

"Okay. Does it say where?"

Hannover looked at Jackie.

"I'm trying to find out who killed Grover Gilmore down at the Palmer Wildlife Habitat Park, Matt," Jackie explained. "I'm not trying to scoop Bingo. I'd be happy to turn over the information exclusive to the *Chronicle* as soon as I come up with a name. The thing is, I'm leaving town for two weeks in two days. If I can't help pin down who this killer is before then, then I won't be able to do anything until I come back."

"How does that affect me?" Matt Hannover asked.

"I thought you might sleep safer knowing that a killer is off the streets."

Hannover gave Jackie another look. "I am a third-degree black belt. I could paralyze your arms without even touching you."

"Woof."

"Who's that?"

Jackie turned to introduce Jake, now standing in the doorway.

"He's my dog."

"Protective, eh?"

Jackie shrugged. "I'm still walking around."

Hannover looked at the screen, fiddled a bit. "Allen's heading to a bar called Ann & Mal's, near Beakins Park."

"Thank you." Jackie prepared to go.

Hannover then handed her a roll of computer paper. "Do you want to take this?"

"What is it?"

"Bingo asked me to pull some facts for him," Hannover said flatly. "He didn't say anything about giving you a copy, but I figured since you're going that way anyway, you might as well give it to him. I'll leave it to the dictates of your conscience whether you want to read Bingo's private material or not."

Jackie took the paper from Hannover, prepared to leave, then turned back. "Listen, Matt?"

Hannover turned.

"You ever laugh?"

"What?"

"Do you ever belly-laugh, guffaw, chortle, chuckle, throw back your head and laugh until your sides hurt?"

Hannover slowly shook his head.

"Well, you should start. You'd be halfway cute if you did. Watch this." Jackie put the computer paper down on the floor, bent, and in a few moments achieved a perfect headstand.

"That's . . ." Hannover started to say "not so hard," then realized that actually perhaps it was. "How do you do that?"

Jackie backed out of it, not quite as gracefully as she would have liked, but without falling over either, and then instructed.

"Get up."

Hannover did. He was nearly six feet four, Jackie noticed. While height wasn't all that important to Jackie, there was a certain advantage, she knew, to being able to change a lightbulb without a chair. "Take off the duck hunter's vest."

"Duck hunters don't wear vests like this," Hannover frowned critically.

"Shh," Jackie said, doing her best Mel Blanc. "Be veh-wy, veh-wy qwiet."

Hannover took off his vest and neatly hung it on the back of his chair.

Jackie was impressed. "All right, crouch down." Hannover did as instructed.

"Hands flat on the floor about two feet apart."

Hannover obliged.

"Now slowly straighten your leg, keeping your hands flat. That's right, shift your weight forward. Now do this slowly—you're going to lift yourself up so that your knees are resting on the triceps of your arms."

Hannover achieved the position with a minimum of trouble.

"Now you're going to slowly straighten your legs straight up to the ceiling, shifting most of the weight to your head. Your hands and arms are just for balance. Go a little bit more . . . higher. I've got your leg, come on. Bring up the other one. Now, I'm going to let go. Ready?"

"Okay," Hannover said, his face contorted with tension.

"Go ahead and breathe. There's plenty of oxygen down there."

Hannover breathed and finally, proud although upside down, was standing on his head.

"Now," Jackie said, noticing with approval that the rugby shirt was sliding down, revealing the computer maven's well-toned midriff. "Try not to laugh . . ."

Still chuckling to herself over how hysterical poor Matt had gotten when she started tickling him, Jackie pulled out of the *Chronicle* parking lot and almost collided with Felix Cruz.

"What the hell are you . . . !" The gaunt police detective bolted out of his car and ran over to Jackie's driver's side window.

The film instructor was about to plead that she was rushing to comfort a sick mother when the two

former partners in crime-solving recognized each
other. "Felix!"

"Jackie!"

Leaning out the window, Jackie gave the homicide lieutenant an awkward hug. Normally, she
wasn't this affectionate, but Jackie wasn't above putting herself out to beat a ticket.

"Long time no see."

"I've been calling you . . ."

"I know," Jackie said quickly, imagining that between her turning off her cellular phone for long
periods of time, and not always checking in for messages at home and at work, that there were probably
all sorts of people she owed phone calls.

"I just wanted to say . . ." The stern, mostly un-
emotional policeman struggled for words. "I just
want to tell you, Jackie," Cruz said finally, "that I
am in your debt for the great and humanitarian
service you rendered my son, Eduardo. Oh, and my
wife. And if there is ever anything I can do to repay
you for your help, it would be my honor."

"The pleasure was mine, Felix," Jackie said at
once. "Really, it was nothing. Now, listen. I'm trying
to help solve this case at the zoo . . ."

"Wonderful." Cruz clapped his hands together.
"We can certainly use your assistance. We need all
the help we can get."

"I sure could use a police escort and the power
of your badge to get a few answers."

"Well, madam," Cruz said, "it seems hardly fair
that in helping you to help me that I should discharge
my debt to you. But I accept, without question."

"Let's ride," Jackie instructed.

CHAPTER 21

At the Palmer Wildlife Habitat Park, a figure pulled himself up out of the pile of fertilizer that Maury had investigated earlier in the week and made his way for the Aviary-Simian House.

All his life Albert Schweitzer Woltzer had done the very best he could to be a good cop, a good man, and an asset to his community. But sometimes Albert had fallen short.

After losing his job with the Palmer Police Department, Albert's nagging alcohol dependency had worsened considerably, and as a result his life had deteriorated.

Now Albert lived in the woods near Beakins Park. He wasn't very comfortable there, but his panhandling efforts allowed him to get enough cheap booze every night to drink himself insensible, and when you are insensible, you don't mind much of anything. One night, however, when Albert was unable to get himself together even to the point where he could shamble down to the entrance to the Hab-

itat Wildlife Park, he had overheard something that
had changed his life.

He had heard some people discussing how some
animal was killing people. It was sick, Woltzer had
heard—not sick enough to die, but sick enough to
make people sick. The zookeeper, what was his
name? Grover, that was it. Grover had always been
nice to Albert, letting him use the toilet in the bathroom, and giving him fruit to eat from the animal
food bins—not like that horrible kid who chased
him with a shovel when he tried to steal a piece of
meat.

Anyway, Albert had heard Grover begging his
boss, Mr. Slake, to put the gorilla in isolation, but
the mean old politician had refused. He said that
he wouldn't take the chance of removing the gorilla
because Gooey was one of the biggest attractions in
the zoo—all the kids came to see him especially—
and Slake wasn't going to give those sons of guns in
City Hall an excuse to fire him and close the zoo so
they could open their gosh-darn theme park.

Woltzer had been dumbstruck. How could they
do that? Let the gorilla who was making people sick
stay right out in an open cage like that?

Grover had told Woltzer that the same thing had
happened in Philadelphia several years ago, and finally a group of concerned citizens had been forced
to sue the zoo, in order to get it to take the animal
out of circulation.

Grover had tried to get someone, anyone, to listen, but everyone, it seemed, was in on the fix. Finally, it was Albert himself who had remembered

from the old days that Marcella Jacobs, that very pretty newswoman on TV, had worked in Philadelphia during the time the whole zoo fiasco was going on. She, if anybody, would understand that it was an important story.

Grover had gotten Marcella to come down, but then he had been killed by that ostrich. Albert wasn't sure who killed Sadie and got Beau so mad that he killed Grover Gilmore. He had been sick and passed out when it had happened. However, Albert had a pretty good idea. There weren't all that many people who had both motive and opportunity. The problem was, no one would ever listen to a drunk like Albert Woltzer, no one but Michael McGowan, perhaps, and he was out of town.

Woltzer decided that he would have to take a chance. He had been avoiding the policemen who'd been going in and out of the zoo, out of both fear and embarrassment. They'd probably suspect that he might know something, because he hung around the place so much. He hated the idea of getting mixed up in this business. But he sure felt bad about poor Grover.

Now Albert decided he would do one thing in memory of Grover. Once and for all he would do what he was no longer allowed to do for the police force: stop a killer.

CHAPTER 22

As they sped along West Elm, Jackie had a big smile on her face. Lieutenant Cruz had agreed to ride in Jackie's Jeep. He would go through the printouts for her while she zipped to the Palmer Pet Pals Hospital. It was literally a license to speed.

"You know, Jackie," Cruz commented with as much restraint as possible. "You drive much too fast."

"Remember, Felix," Jackie commented as she downshifted a second and then a third time. "I saved your son's life."

"Yes . . ."

Giving Jackie the flashing red light to put on the roof of her car had not been Lieutenant Cruz's idea, needless to say. Indeed, it broke every law in the book. Still, she had saved his beloved son, Eduardo.

"Hang on." Jackie took a corner so fast that the tires screeched.

She had also, Cruz feebly reminded himself, saved his wife.

"I wish we had the siren," Jackie brooded, cutting off a fire truck.

"Did you see this list of schoolchildren?" Cruz asked, vainly trying to keep his mind off the landscape now zipping by like an Impressionist painting.

"Yes," Jackie answered tersely. She was trying to pass the car in front of her. "Apparently only the children who actually touched the animals got sick. There doesn't seem to be much of an incubation period, so I'm going to assume now that the zoo is closed . . ."

Cruz nodded. The zoo had now been closed for three days. Clearly if the Palmer Group had their way, it would never reopen.

"I think we can assume that anyone who is not already sick is out of the woods," Jackie finished.

"That is a relief," Cruz said at once. "I would chance myself getting sick, but I could not risk bringing this horrible disease home to my wife and son." Jackie, with a burst of speed and a blast of the horn, finally pulled ahead.

"I think it was one of the simians," she said abruptly.

"Yes?"

"Woof."

"Jake agrees."

"Yes," Felix Cruz commented. "But perhaps one of you two can explain it to me."

"Simply put . . ."

"Yes?" Lieutenant Cruz prompted her impatiently.

"Everyone who got sick visited the Aviary-Simian

House," Jackie explained. "They visited other buildings, but no group visited exactly the same ones. Second, the animals who are dead, Sadie the ostrich and Jethrine the ape . . ."

"The mother of the little gorilla," Felix Cruz remembered. "And the wife of that ape Irv, I guess."

"Right," Jackie agreed. "They're dead. Somebody or something killed them. Then there are three humans. One took sick after leaving the Simian House. One collapsed near death *in* the Simian House. And one was killed by an escaped animal in the Simian House. What did you learn in police school about one time fate, two times coincidence, and . . . ?"

"Three times spells a pattern," Cruz finished. "You know something like this happened in Philadelphia two years ago."

"Really?" Jackie asked. "People died from a mysterious illness?"

"Yes." The careful police lieutenant quickly scanned the computer paper pages. "Japanese tourists that time. They were very upset of course. The zoo officials figured out which animal was the carrier of this disease and were about to destroy it when an animal rights group, led by Ray . . . I can't read this name here."

"Rayburn Herman?" Jackie asked.

"That's it. They stopped them."

"Quite a coincidence," Jackie muttered.

"What's that?" Cruz asked.

Jackie told him about her visit to *The Jerry Waring Show.*

• • •

Ann & Mal's was a young person's bar. Not trendy, not famous for its food, just a laid-back local bar. If there were any surfers in Palmer, they would have hung out there.

The bartender, Terry Bishop, a long-haired, mustachioed fellow, tended bar most evenings unless a good rock band was playing somewhere in the area, in which case he was in his VW van heading that way. He greeted Jackie with a smile.

"Hey, Terry." Jackie sat on a red cracked-leather stool and helped herself to a cracker and some port wine cheese from a brown ceramic crock. "What's happening?"

"Nothing much. Have you heard the latest? They're tearing down the zoo and putting up a theme park."

"Really?" Jackie was amazed. "Who are they going to get to take over for Morton Slake as supervisor?"

"Lew Perkins," Bishop answered. "He's sitting right over there with his stockbroker. That's how I found out—the waitress overheard."

Jackie took another sip of her drink. It did make sense, of course. Lew Perkins not only had experience with animals, but also had served in city government during Big Bill Curtis's administration.

Jackie got up to go over to their booth and talk to him, but Felix Cruz signaled to her.

Jackie turned to Bishop and requested, "Do me a favor? Keep an eye on Mr. Perkins over there. I need to talk to him later. If he shows any signs of leaving, would you let me know?"

"Sure," Bishop agreed, taking the change that Jackie had left for him and throwing it into a small glass pitcher next to the cash register. "How's Petey?"

"Good. How's Billy?"

"Pretty good," Terry answered. "But he had a little mini-disaster the other day. Some jerks over in Wardville broke into my van and looted it. He lost some of his hockey equipment. He's missing a leg pad and he's got a big match against Tonnington next week. These things aren't cheap and with what I spent on fixing the van up and replacing the spare and stuff, I just can't afford it. He's pretty upset."

"I can let you have a goalie's leg pad," Jackie said.

"What?!"

"Peter's got an extra one," Jackie explained. "It's not in great shape, you may have to tape it up a little."

"Hey, that much I can handle," Bishop responded.

"Well then, it's yours if you want it," Jackie said graciously. "Stop over my house on your way home. It's sitting out on the front porch."

"Great. Thanks, Jackie!"

Felix Cruz came over. "I found Mr. Allen. He's in a booth in the back with Dr. Humphries."

They walked over to the table in the back, near the moose head whose red eyes lit up whenever anyone entered or exited the doors to the bathroom.

"Hey, glad you finally tracked me down," Allen uncordially greeted her.

"We did the best we could, Charles," Jackie snapped. "We have families—our own families—to worry about."

"Eduardo," Felix Cruz explained, "is all right. Thanks to Ms. Walsh here."

"Thanks to my dogs, you mean," Jackie smiled.

"Woof."

"Well, actually only Jake is my dog. Maury belongs to Marcella. I was lucky enough to draw baby-sitting duty while she was in the hospital."

"Who is this Eduardo?" Lee Humphries, the medical examiner, asked the handsome Dominican detective. "Not to be nosy—and remembering of course that when the coroner's never heard of you that's good news . . ."

"Eduardo is my beloved son," Cruz replied. "Here." He reached for his wallet and pulled out the snapshot fold. "This is Eduardo. And this is his grandmother, my mother . . . and his grandfather, my father . . . And my wife . . . I'm sorry. I hope I'm not boring you."

"No, it's a pleasure to look at nice pictures," Lee said at once. "You should see some of the photographs we get in my line of work. Enough to turn your stomach."

"I'll say," Bingo Allen chimed in, forcing down another tempura-covered vegetable. "I'll tell you, those pictures of Morton Slake . . ."

"Please," Jackie requested.

"Some sort of virus," Lee said, shaking her head. "I've done a lot of autopsies. Violent deaths from every cause you can imagine. And some you can't.

It's only a handful of cases that really frighten me. I can take any of the natural stuff. Anything, that is, but the strange animal-carried viruses. They give me the willies.''

"Me too," Jackie agreed. "What can we do to avoid something like this happening to us?"

"Keep yourself and your surroundings cold and dry," Humphries advised. "They prefer a warm, moist environment."

"Did you hear about Albert Woltzer?" Bingo then asked.

Jackie was momentarily nonplussed.

"Didn't you see *The Jerry Waring Show?*" Bingo jogged her memory.

Now Jackie remembered. "Oh, I was there—but I left early. What happened?"

The waitress interjected while setting down their drinks. "I taped it, if you want to watch it."

"That would be good," Jackie said. "Could you put it on in here?" She pointed to a television in the corner.

"Coming right up."

"All I know," Woltzer said, "was whoever was supposed to keep these people and animals safe was not doing their job, and the gorilla—the little gorilla with the flu or whatever he's got—shoulda been taken out of there long ago."

Jackie looked at the image on the screen and knew at once that something was wrong. After a moment she saw what it was. The image of Albert Woltzer wasn't moving at all. Apparently they had found some still photo of Woltzer from an earlier time and were putting that on the screen now while the former hero cop's voice was heard from far off.

In fact, from the crackles and breaks in the sound transmission, Jackie realized that Woltzer was probably talking to Jerry Waring from a public telephone.

"So, Mr. Woltzer," Jerry Waring's voice was heard off-screen. "You strongly believe that poor little Gooey the gorilla should be taken out of public circulation?"

"One way or . . ."

Waring cut off Woltzer. His image faded from the screen and the camera focused back on Jerry Waring and Rayburn Herman.

"What about that *suggestion*, Mr. Herman?" Waring pushed. "Do you think Gooey the baby gorilla should be locked away in some dark tomb never again to see the light of day?"

"Of course not," Herman said. "This is a classic case of blaming the victim. Gooey should not be stripped of his few creature comforts because of yet another human foul-up.

"Apparently this contaminated blood was given to the poor ape's mother after a difficult delivery. It killed her. It left Gooey an orphan, so starved for attention he keeps reaching out to any human being who's nice to him. With tragic consequences, we must admit, but the answer here is treatment, not isolation. I think we owe this poor little guy an apology . . ."

"And the bottom line is," Jerry Waring pounced.

Jackie noticed that the host looked a lot taller on television than in real life.

"You would sue the city," Waring continued, "to keep this gorilla where he is. Is *that* what you're saying?"

"If that's what it takes . . ." Herman started to say.

Jackie turned off the TV. "We should go."

Cruz looked at Dr. Humphries and then queried, "But are we done here? I wanted to ask the doctor a few questions."

"Me too," Bingo said.

"Why don't we do this, then?" Jackie proposed. "We'll walk over to the zoo. Make sure Gooey, our little material witness, is okay. Then we'd better find some way to put him in protective custody."

"A gorilla?" Lee Humphries asked.

Jackie shrugged. "He's got a lot of enemies right now. People he made sick. Zoo and city officials who stand to face crippling lawsuits and probably would love to see Gooey disappear so nobody could conclusively prove that he was the Typhoid Mary who started this epidemic."

"That's a lot of potential suspects you're throwing around," Bingo Allen pointed out.

"This may be dangerous," Cruz added.

"Let's go—whoever's going," Jackie said. "And let's pick up Mr. Perkins on the way out."

CHAPTER 23

Night fell on the Palmer Wildlife Habitat Park like a waterfall of black velvet. Jackie had been in the zoo many times, at least a half a dozen times after dark. She had never been frightened before. It wouldn't have occurred to her that any of the animals could get out of their cages.

Now they were all out of their cages.

Someone had released the animals.

"Woof!" Jake reassured his mistress, letting her know he was next to her.

Jackie used her cellular phone to make a few calls.

"Jackie. Jackie! Do I have to set my dog on you?!"

Jackie turned and saw Marcella Jacobs approaching with Maury.

"Marcy!"

The two women clasped and held on to each other.

At the same time, Jake and Maury exchanged doggy greetings.

"What on earth is happening?" Marcella demanded.

"You wouldn't believe it if I told you," Jackie responded. "Come on. Let's keep moving. There's got to be some lights somewhere."

As they walked slowly and carefully through the park, the two friends filled each other in on what the other didn't know.

Marcella told Jackie that Sadie had been examined by prominent Palmer vet Jason Huckle and he had discovered no trace of any virus. Indeed Sadie had probably not been sick at all. The surprising thing was, Sadie was pregnant—a very unusual occurrence among ostriches in captivity. Further, Huckle managed to establish that Sadie had been bludgeoned with an object more resembling a thin-faced hammer than a golf club.

Jackie told Marcella that as she'd entered the park, the realization about the great escape of the animals had caused Felix Cruz and the new head of the zoo, Lewis Perkins, to go running off to see if they could help recapture the wandering beasts. At the same time, Bingo Allen had run off in another direction to gather facts for the story and Lee Humphries had followed along.

Jackie, not knowing whether she should remain in this dangerous area—after all, an accidental contact with Gooey the affectionate gorilla alone could land her in the hospital—had decided to stay where she was for the moment.

All of a sudden she stopped short.

"What is it, Jackie?" Marcella demanded. "From

the expression on your face, either you just had a brainstorm or you're about to lay an egg. Either way, I'll bet it's a helluva story."

Jackie grabbed Marcella's arm.

"Ow. Careful, I've got major bruises."

"Sorry." Jackie let go and at the same time noticed that someone stood in front of them in the gloom. "Thalia!" she called out.

The portly older woman approached cautiously, holding in her hand a small flashlight, and a large Colt .45. "Who's there?"

"Jackie. And Marcella. And Maury."

"Maury's there?" Thalia asked. The dog trainer extraordinaire loved Maury. To her he was the perfect "other person's dog"—big, sloppy, affectionate, and absolutely no threat to ever be in an obedience trial against her beagle Clematis. "Look, Clematis," she cooed to her beagle in a bag, "it's Maury."

Maury immediately came right over, noticed the beagle shaking uncontrollably in Ms. Gilmore's woven straw shoulder bag, and reached out his paw to say hi.

"That's quite a gun you have there, Thalia," Jackie pointed out calmly.

"Well, yes," Thalia answered matter-of-factly. "I don't have a big dog to defend me, so I rely on my grandfather's dogleg Colt."

"Have you ever fired that thing?" Marcella asked doubtfully.

Thalia nodded grimly. "Benjamin, my late husband, taught me how to be a dead shot with this."

All of a sudden there was a rustling in the bushes.

Thalia swiveled and fired from her hip, watching the branches over Albert Woltzer's head disappear.

"Wait!" the alcoholic former policeman pleaded. "Don't shoot!"

"Come on out of there," Thalia ordered, "with your hands on top of your head. One false move out of you and I'll fill you so full of lead . . ."

"Better get out of the park, Albert," Jackie advised. "Someone let all the animals loose."

Wild-haired and grimy, Woltzer nodded. "It was the zoo guard."

"Are you sure?" Marcella asked.

"Yeah, I saw him," Woltzer stated. "He used his master key."

"Have you seen Gooey, the little gorilla?" Jackie asked. "Is he loose?"

"Nah," Woltzer answered.

"Are you sure?" Marcella asked.

"Yeah," Woltzer answered. "See for yourself."

He then turned back the way he came, as if signaling the others to follow. Marcella and Jackie exchanged looks and then both women turned to Thalia.

"I'm game if you are," she said.

The Simian House was not empty. Many of the animals and birds, frightened, perhaps, at the prospect of the unknown world outside, had chosen to stay in their cages.

The Simian House now looked very strange indeed. The room was full of steam, for one thing. As simians of different stripes and breeds looked down at them, Jackie noticed the blistering paint, the fogged windows, and Gooey, a curled-up ball of wet fur lying near a floor grate. It appeared that he had met his end from a burst from the hot water hose, which lay on the floor near the long radiator on the left side of the house.

"Who did this, do you think?" Marcella asked. "The guard?"

Woltzer shrugged. "Guess you won't be able to ask him."

"Why not?" Marcella asked.

"He's in the next room."

Marcella went at once into the aviary.

Thalia followed carefully.

Jackie turned to Woltzer and asked him quietly, "Did anyone see you do this?"

"No one but them," Woltzer answered, indicating his silent simian accusers staring at them from every corner of the room.

"I wonder how they feel about it," Jackie commented.

"It's the law of the jungle," Woltzer responded before exiting into the night. "Whoever has the top hand uses it. They understand that part of it."

Jackie nodded, and walked to the doorway.

Marcella, crouched over the sprawled body of the guard, didn't bother to turn around. "He may have killed Gooey, but he didn't get far."

Jackie looked quickly, then turned away, a little green. "Who did this? Beau, again?"

Marcella shook her head. "No, I'd recognize that guy's handiwork. Somebody stoved this guy's head in with a hammer or something. Maybe they wanted it to look like an ostrich did it, but they didn't do a very good job."

All of a sudden they heard a strange whirring sound. Looking at each other in speechless horror, the three women shrank back.

Hoss Greenaway, wild-eyed and holding a bloody hammer, sat in his top-of-the-line wheelchair like a king on a throne.

"Well, hello, Carly. We meet again."

Marcella kept her distance and warily eyed the young killer as he pressed a button and rolled toward her. "Hoss. Long time no see."

"Sorry you couldn't get over to the house. Your friend there was nice enough to bring me your gift."

Marcella dodged past Hoss's mechanical chair and managed to get him to turn slightly so that his back was to Jackie. "Obviously you're a remarkable young man, Horace. To get yourself over here, in the condition you're in. And to manage to kill the guard. Did you make him open the cages first, to cover your tracks? So people would assume it was another animal attack?"

"Yeah, I killed him. Actually, he was so drunk it was easy. I tried to make it look like Beau did it, but I guess it wouldn't even fool a layman, would it?"

"Murder is harder than it looks," Marcella pointed out calmly.

"It is, if you have to pull the trigger yourself," Hoss agreed. "The first time I got our deceased friend there to do my dirty work. Cost me a few bucks too. He was kind of a sadist, anyway. Figures they'd put him to work in here, right?''

"Why did you have Sadie killed, Hoss?" Marcella asked.

While Hoss formulated his answer, Thalia tried to switch off the safety on her gun, but found it was hopelessly jammed. Jackie, very slowly, peered into the room where Maury was munching on a banana someone had left in one of the empty cages, and tried to signal the noble pup to come closer.

"Nasty bird," Hoss replied. "And you could see what was going to happen. The moment it had its eggs, there would be a media circus. Gooey would be taken out and put somewhere else, then Old Man Slake would have bowed to the pressure from everyone and had the poor little guy put to sleep."

"You didn't know that," Marcella said. "They might have been able to send him somewhere to get cured."

"No," Hoss conceded. "And I checked that out. Even offered to pay for it myself, but no. They were afraid to death of lawsuits. They figured if they killed him and buried the body where nobody would ever find it, then no one could ever sue them. Pretty naive, huh? Thinking that people wouldn't sue unless they had a good strong case. There would have been people flying in here from three states, claiming they deserved a bundle because they were thinking they might have come by here sometime, and they might have gotten sick, so therefore they'd have to be paid off for what might have happened to them. And it was all lies."

"Is it lies that Morton Slake is dead and that little

girl is in the hospital, Hoss?" Marcella asked.

"Well, I don't know about that," Hoss conceded. "I got my suspicions, though. How come if everyone who touches Gooey gets sick, I didn't get sick? How come the guard didn't get sick? Or Grover?"

"I think the guard did get sick, Hoss," Marcella responded. "He looked like death the last time I saw him."

"He looks like death now too, doesn't he?" Hoss replied nastily.

"That's right," Marcella agreed quietly. "But you actually wasted your time, Hoss. Chances are, untreated as he was, he would have died of natural causes before ever getting a chance to finger you."

"Bull," Hoss responded. "Besides, even if that was true, I couldn't take that chance. I would have killed him sooner but Beau did a lot worse to me than I anticipated."

"How did you know Beau would kill Grover?" Marcella asked.

"I didn't know," Hoss snickered. "I got lucky. I was kind of hoping he would get you, actually."

"So you recognized me, even in disguise?" Marcella pushed him.

Desperate, Jackie gestured again in Maury's direction.

The big dog waved his tail hello, but did not come over. He was busy sniffing monkey perches.

"Yeah, well, you aren't exactly Alec Guinness, are you?" Hoss sneered.

"I guess not," Marcella responded.

"I was mad at you, Ms. Jacobs," Hoss continued,

"for treating me like a lump of animal stuff—but then I'm used to that. Grover used to treat me the same way. He'd pretend to be patient with me, but I could see the contempt in his eyes. He knew that the only reason I had this job was because my dad has clout with City Hall. Why do you suppose they put me in the cold room? They were hoping I'd get so miserable, I'd quit. But I stuck it out. Hell, I outlasted them all."

"You did indeed, Hoss," Marcella agreed. "And you were lucky that you were given duty in the cold room. That probably is what kept Gooey from making you sick."

Hoss grew lachrymose. "He was a good little guy, Gooey. Always hugging me. Always happy to see me when I came by. Grover would chase me away, because he couldn't stand the fact that the little guy liked me better than he did him."

Marcella shook her head. "Hoss, you've got this all wrong. Grover probably already suspected by the time that you started working here that Gooey was the one who was making everybody sick. He made a special effort to keep from touching or being touched by the gorilla and he tried to warn away anyone who got too near."

"Lies. All lies," Hoss yelled, suddenly realizing that what Marcella was telling him might be true. "They were jealous of the little guy because he got too much attention. Because his father was famous. That's all. They would have killed him, if I hadn't stopped them."

Marcella shook her head. "Hoss, this little ape

was worth tens of thousands of dollars. They would have moved heaven and earth to save him.

"Grover and some of the others only wanted to get him into a pet hospital where he could be treated and where he wouldn't make any more human beings sick. Your protecting him got Grover killed, got Morton Slake killed, and now got the guard killed. And now what? Will you kill me? And Jackie and Thalia, and anyone else who might see you here tonight? The park is crawling with policemen. Do you really think they're going to let you roll on out of here carrying a bloody hammer without saying anything to you?"

"I've got lawyers. My dad's got lawyers. I'll claim I was on drugs or something. They can't touch me!" Hoss shouted. He then moved to the door. "All right. I'm leaving. You're right. It won't do me any good to kill you evil witches. But if you think I'm not going to get away with this, you've got another think coming. And I'm still just a kid. I've got a lot of years to plan and scheme and put the pieces in place to get even with you, lady. And someday, someday when you least expect it, you'll get yours."

Hoss dropped the bloody hammer to the ground and prepared to take his leave. His path was blocked by the father of the little gorilla he had befriended. Old Irv did not allow Hoss to plead his case, to cop a plea, or to find a judge amenable to a whopping bribe. He simply reached out, picked Horace Greenaway the Third up out of his chair, hugged him and squeezed with all his might.

Marcella screamed and Jackie, who felt like doing

the same, managed to form a word.

"Jake!"

Marcella then screamed, "Maury!" And the two dogs appeared at once, barking furiously and placing themselves between their mistresses and the avenging ape.

Irv considered fighting the lot, then gave it up. He was an old ape. He couldn't take on the whole world anymore. At this point in his life, he was barely able to run away.

EPILOGUE

The Palmer Wildlife Habitat Park ended with a bang, not a whimper. A company was hired to demolish the former zoo, and a herd of animal rights activists, led by Rayburn Herman, were there to cheer as the bulldozers and wrecking balls knocked down each of the former animal prison buildings and cleared them away.

Jane Bellamy continued to weather the storms of controversy regarding her stewardship of the city, and successfully fought back a recall effort. Corky Dole, able to close the case without embarrassing any living person, also managed to hold on as district attorney.

Jerry Waring showed amazing restraint in the aftermath of the entire zoo debacle. He'd run an occasional feature as a zoo animal, hiding in someone's toolshed, was finally rounded up and brought to the Wardville Zoo, where the animals would be temporarily housed until they could find a new home. The fact that he was given so much credit in solving the murder (at the expense of Jackie, who was barely mentioned, as usual) helped his ratings, and insured that Jerry Waring would stick around to poke his electronic nose in everyone's business for the next few years to come.

Albert Woltzer's role in the whole affair was downplayed and he vanished, leaving people to wonder whether he would resurface in some other hobo camp or whether this time he was gone for good.

Beau vanished as well.

Marcella Jacobs returned to work something of a hero, and was not shy to point out to her superiors how she had managed to crack a story, lying flat on her back, that her would-be replacements hadn't come close to reporting.

Maury, the hero dog, was given a T-bone steak as big as his head, but then was quietly banned from the new Teen Skaters Theme Park. Everyone knew that the giant puppy meant well, but no one was going to be able to afford insurance if the big lug wasn't kept from destroying everything in sight.

Jackie and Jake? Well, they just quietly chalked up another job well done, and then quietly drove down to Florida with Ronald Dunn. For these two intrepid crimefighters, the spotlight and the adulation of the media were not necessary. They were just happy to keep things running smoothly in their happy little town.